Another Second Chance

Masters of the Prairie Winds Club
Book Eight

by Avery Gale

Copyright © 2017 by Avery Gale
ISBN 978-1-944472-43-6
All cover art and logo © Copyright 2017 by Avery Gale
All rights reserved.

The Masters of the Prairie Winds Club® and Avery Gale® are registered trademarks

Cover Design by Jess Buffett
Published by Avery Gale

Thank you for respecting the hard work of this author.

This is a work of fiction. Names, places, characters and incidents either are the product of the author's imagination or are used fictitiously and any resemblance to any actual persons, living or dead, organizations, events or locales are entirely coincidental.

No part of this book may be reproduced, stored in a retrieval system, or transmitted by any means without the written permission of the author and publishing company.

WARNING: The unauthorized reproduction or distribution of this copyrighted work is illegal. Criminal copyright infringement, including infringement without monetary gain, is investigated by the FBI and is punishable by up to 5 years in federal prison and a fine of $250,000.

If you find any books being sold or shared illegally, please contact the author at avery.gale@ymail.com.

Dedication

I'm able to write humor because my cousins, Karen Bailey and Cathy Bryant, let me be ridiculous and they encourage me to be myself when the rest of the world insists on conformity.

My books have amazing covers because Jess Buffett at Sinfully Sweet Designs can take the tiny bits of information I give her and turn it into the perfect cover. How she manages to see into my imagination is still a mystery and should probably scare her.

And last, but by no means least, Sandy Ebel at Personal Touch Editing, took my stream of conscious writing and whipped it into shape. I appreciate her suggestions and attention to detail more than I can tell you.

Prologue

One year ago

LIAM JAMES WATCHED through the one-way glass in amusement as Guinevere Colbert-Lister rolled her brilliant-blue, aristocratic eyes when his boss turned his attention to his laptop. The petite beauty continued to swing her legs and glare periodically at the floor as if it had intentionally distanced itself from the bottoms of her scuffed, leather boots. Her honey blonde hair fell in a curtain of waves to her waist and an image of his hand fisted in the blonde silk flashed in his mind, sending a surge of blood to his cock. The strands were a hundred shades of spun gold, but it would all have to go—it was far too recognizable. *Nobody who sees her hair would ever forget it. Every straight man I know would have the same fantasies I'm having.*

The door behind him opened and he nodded when his long-time partner, Bode Ford, finally stepped into the small, dimly lit room.

"Christ, Tiffany has been asking me questions about us transitioning to another organization." Tiffany was the receptionist for their floor. She looked to be in her early thirties, but there were times when Liam wondered if her age and I.Q. weren't too close together.

"What the fuck? *Transitioning?* Don't tell me. She

signed up for some word of the day email and that's today's word." Liam chuckled at Bode's frustration because it was a sentiment they shared. Tiffany was the boss's niece and they all knew *exactly* how she'd gotten her job. What no one could fathom was how she'd managed to stay on past her probationary period.

If you wanted to put a picture in the slang dictionary next to the term ditzy, you'd do well to use Tiffany's. Liam had yet to ask her to do something she hadn't fucked up; the only consistent thing about her was her inconsistency. In his opinion, the biggest problem with Tiffany was her relentless pursuit of both him and Bode. Had you asked him a year ago if he could ever see himself filing a sexual harassment complaint against a beautiful female co-worker, Liam would have thought you'd gone off the deep end. But he and Bode had both hit the end of their patience after the office Christmas party last week. Tiffany's blatant sexual aggression had made everyone around them uncomfortable, and they'd abandoned any hope they could tactfully avoid her.

The morning after the party, they'd called Kyle and Kent West and accepted their offer to join the Prairie Winds team, promising their supervisor they would stick around long enough to finish up the human trafficking case. Now, thanks to Ms. Colbert-Lister's tip, they were closer than ever to wrapping it up. After arranging for her transfer to the Witness Protection Program, they would start packing.

"I'm not thrilled about Tiffany using that particular term. I don't even want to think about what the other Masters at the Prairie Winds Club will think if they get wind of it. And why the fuck is she privy to human re-sources information which should have been *need to know* only?"

Liam knew if he didn't shut him down, Bode would wind himself up to the point he was so pissed off, he'd scare the woman on the other side of the glass into silence, and they needed her cooperation. That was if their boss ever decided she'd cooled her heels long enough to agree to what she was facing. When Liam didn't take the bait about their new team, Bode blew out a breath and turned his attention to the petite blonde who'd started pacing the length of the small room.

"Does she realize the danger she's in? If nothing else, they'll want to make an example of her." Bode hadn't taken his eyes off her even though he was speaking to Liam. When he reached forward and switched on the microphone in the interrogation room, the first sound they heard was her huff out a breath of obvious frustration.

"I don't think so. She's still under the impression her usual bodyguard will be able to protect her." Liam had listened as their boss tried in vain to explain, tactfully, the seriousness of her situation, but his words had fallen on deaf ears. Her irate muttering finally came over the speakers after Liam cranked the volume up far enough to hear the whoosh of air as she stormed past the hidden mic.

"They could have at least left me with my phone. I could read or something. Keme Meadows's new book is smokin'. Dammit, those two guys with the panty-dropping smiles foisted me off on Toad Face so fast, you'd think I had a disease or something. I can't just sit in here and stare at the walls waiting for Froggy to come back. I need a distraction."

Liam felt his mouth drop open and when he turned to Bode, his expression reflected the same surprise.

"The two hotties leave me to Frogman and bolt. Some

things never change."

"Fucking hell. She's talking about us."

Well, at least Bode had finally forgotten about Tiffany. Thank God.

"I can't even remember the last time a woman called me a hottie. Jesus, I feel old." Liam watched her stalk from one end of the small room to other, her steps so precise, he wondered if she was unconsciously counting them. The woman was gorgeous, but there was something off about her, and so far, he hadn't been able to pinpoint what it was. Maybe it was the boots? They looked well-worn and too scuffed to be a fashion statement.

"Has anyone figured out why she was at the track?" Bode's chuckle drew Liam's attention away from the agitated beauty who was now doing some kind of yoga stretch which was probably illegal in half the counties in England.

"Evidently, our little debutante is a closet gearhead. Much to her parents' frustration, she loves all things mechanical. What the Queen's cousin and his wife don't know is her interest isn't reserved to watching the races from the sideline. She loves hanging out in the garages, watching the mechanics work." When Liam raised his brow in question, Bode shook his head. "She isn't a groupie. What I mean is she's genuinely interested in the inner workings of the cars, not the men working on them. By all accounts, she's a hell of a mechanic."

Liam was more than a little surprised by Bode's response. Christ, the woman's blood was as blue as the fucking summer sky over the rolling hills of the Glens of Atrim.

Damn, he missed the beauty of Ireland. He didn't have any reason to visit the small village he had grown up in now that his parents were no longer there. That didn't mean he didn't miss the narrow cobblestone and brick streets and brightly painted buildings he'd once called home.

Colbie hoisted herself up onto the table, and it was easy to see she was fast approaching her limit. When she started swinging her legs, Liam smiled. Damn, if she didn't look like a petulant teenager. Her eyes went glassy with unshed years, and he noted the flush coloring her cheeks. Guinevere Colbert-Lister was on the verge of losing her battle to stay calm, and Liam was fighting one of his own. He wanted nothing more than to steal her away from the matronly woman who'd entered the room. As the caseworker assigned to her began explaining what was coming, Guinevere's softly spoken words made his heart clench.

"Feathers, my parents are going to be pissed about this."

No, baby, they're going to lose their minds with grief. Being told your only child died helping save a truckload of kidnapped kids headed to the local slave auction will help ease the pain, but it damn well won't eliminate it altogether.

Chapter One

Colbie used the steel-toe of her oil-stained boots to push herself further under the small sports car she was tuning up and prayed the men questioning her boss hadn't heard the creeper's rollers squeak. *Futt-buckers, why didn't I oil those damned things?*

"You don't have a customer who matches this description?" The man's voice sounded familiar, but Colbie was so rattled, she couldn't remember where she'd heard it. She pulled her extension mirror from beside her, hoping she could get a look at the men, but all she could see were black slacks and black leather loafers. *Not helpful. Those are standard issue for every detective, bounty hunter, and thug in the world.*

A large drip of oil plopped onto her forehead before sliding into her spiky, red hair. Evidently, the Universe didn't think her day had already gone far enough south to require penguin crossing signs. Biting her tongue to keep from cursing a blue streak, Colbie resigned herself to dealing with a streak of black sludge adding a bit of goth to her ridiculous rocker look.

It had taken her months to recognize the woman in the mirror after she'd been forced into witness protection. Although her life had been completely turned upside down by her decision to report the conversation she'd overheard, she'd never regretted helping save the teens who'd been locked in a suburban London basement for weeks while waiting for the next auction sponsored by their captors.

She shouldn't have even been at the track that night. She'd promised her parents she wouldn't go to the races, but she hadn't been able to resist when one of the pit crew captains texted her he was shorthanded and asked if she'd like to fill in. During the race, he'd sent her into the cavernous rooms under the stadium looking for a spare rim. Hidden from view behind stacks of chrome, she'd overheard two men discussing their upcoming slave auction. Even though they hadn't given the exact address where the victims were being held, she'd been able to get enough information the police had been able to figure it out. Unfortunately, someone in the local police department identified her before MI6 could whisk her to safety.

Another man's voice brought her out of her musings and this time, chills raced up her spine. This was the man who'd joked he planned to sample the merchandise before the auction. His high-pitched voice was unmistakable, and she fought the shiver she felt moving through her. *Don't move. Don't move. Don't move.*

"You haven't seen a woman who looks like this?" Colbie heard the rustle of papers and could envision the picture Gus was studying, probably the one from her coming out party. She looked like she'd been dipped in phony and rolled in glitter before being dropped into a big pile of ruffled silk. God Almighty, she hated that damned picture, but it was the one the media had plastered on every newscast for days on end. No doubt her mother had given the sappy pose to anyone who asked for it since it was the one picture where they actually looked like they might be related. And if there was a way to twist a situation until it was about her, Maribelle Colbert-Lister would find it.

Long minutes later, Colbie heard Gus walking the men to the door. Evidently, they'd given her boss their contact information. She heard Gus assure them they'd be the first to know if the woman in the picture brought her car in for service. She had to smile because that was a promise she knew Gus could keep. There wasn't a chance in hell Colbie was going to dress up in silk ruffles and show up as a customer, and it would be a cold day in hell when she couldn't fix her own car.

The heavy thud of Gus' enormous boots stopped near the side of the Spitfire she was tuning for its inattentive owner. *If I had a car like this, it would never lack for my attention.* The powder blue roadster was in pristine condition; it only needed a little TLC to make it a complete showstopper. She'd suffered from car-envy in the past, but this little beauty had stolen her heart. Colbie had never made it a secret the Triumph Spitfire was her dream car… she even had pictures of the small classic on the fridge in her apartment. She fantasized about buying the car from the owner who she had yet to meet. The man or woman hadn't even taken time to dust the dash before bringing it in. It should be a crime for the little gem to be dirty.

"Are you going to come out, or am I going to have to pull you out from under there?" Gus' voice always sounded gruff, but this time, she could hear real frustration in his tone. Not a good sign. She slid out from under the car and let him give her a hand up. His eyes were filled with concern, and she felt herself cringe when she remembered her oil-smeared face and hair.

When she pulled the red rag from her back pocket, he shook his head and took it from her fingers. Using a gentle touch, which always surprised her, he dabbed the oil from her face and hair. She'd been worried when she learned the burly garage owner was married to the petite woman who worked at the local newspaper office. She'd had enough experience with reporters in the past to last a lifetime. Colbie knew too well how ruthless they could be.

Every member of the Queen's extended family was trained from infancy to treat all members of the media with polite disdain. *They are never your friend, dear. Remember that.* That had been all Her Majesty had said to her after photos of Guinevere dancing at a party hit the tabloids her freshman year at Oxford. Colbie had been mortified when she discovered the journalism major she'd befriended and who had promised the evening was "off the record" was responsible. It was also the last time she'd trusted anyone even remotely associated with the media... until Julia. She'd laughed when she was first introduced to her boss' wife. The irony of Augustus and Julia wasn't lost on her; evidently, fate has a sense of humor pairing a man and woman named after Augustus and Julius Caesar.

Returning to the moment, she realized Gus was watching her closely. He'd stepped back, but he was studying like a bug under a microscope.

"Where did you go, Colbie? You zoned out. You're usually more self-aware. The dark circles under your eyes tell me you aren't sleeping well which, no doubt, plays into your disconnection. If I had to guess, I'd say this isn't the first time something has happened recently."

He was right. It wasn't the first thing to ping her radar in the past few weeks, but she'd managed to discount the other incidents as either coincidence or products of her own imagination.

"You're going to tattle, aren't you?" she blurted the question out before she could rein in the words. Gus' association with Kent and Kyle West wasn't common knowledge outside the Prairie Winds team. Gus was a retired Army Ranger who still had close ties to friends and associates he made during the time he'd served his country. That close association is what led her to his door when she'd first moved to Texas.

"You bet your ass. Kent and Kyle are a lot bigger than you are, darlin', and I'm scared spitless of Tobi." Colbie had met Tobi West at a couple of local events. The vivacious woman had immediately embraced her, treating her like they were lifelong friends. "Tobi is fiercely loyal and we both know she's appointed herself your guardian angel. She'll bring her whole contingent down on me if anything happens to you." The corners of Gus' mouth tugged up, telling her he wasn't really intimidated by Tobi and her friends, even though she suspected he probably should be.

"Those guys aren't going to give up, Colbie. If they flash your picture around town, someone is going to recognize you underneath all those layers of fluff."

Gus was right, but she was still holding out hope she wouldn't be forced to relocate. The small apartment she had over the garage was perfect, even if it often reeked of exhaust. The outside entrance gave her just enough separation between home and work, and she never had to worry about being on time. There was also a hidden exit in her bedroom closet which led directly into Gus' office. The motion detectors in the passageway sent text alarms to Gus and the West's security team at the club.

She'd learned about the motion detectors the hard way after using the inside route to avoid an early morning Texas thunderstorm. Kent West had skidded into the parking lot a few minutes later, executing a one-eighty which would have made any stunt driver proud. After she explained, he'd given her a phone number to call if she wanted to avoid another "toad strangler." She still remembered being more embarrassed by his riotous laughter when she'd asked why he thought she knew anyone who would strangle a toad. She was still learning the unique language spoken by Texans, but at least she no longer needed an interpreter to go grocery shopping.

"Jesus H. Christ, Colbie, could you please focus for five minutes? The fact you're so distracted worries the shit out of me. You've had your head up your ass for the past week, and these last ten minutes, you've been gone more than you've been present."

She could see the underlying concern in his eyes and held back her smile at his cursing. She'd learned early on that her boss had a tendency to curse when he was frustrated. The colorful language wasn't as large a part of his everyday language as most of the men who frequented the garage, but it sure came to the surface when he'd reached the limit of his patience.

LIAM'S PHONE VIBRATED, repeatedly, on the bench outside the gym's large shower. Stepping out from under the spray, he grabbed a towel and studied the screen. Since he'd muted the annoying device, he knew there were only a few people whose calls could activate the sound. Looking at the screen, Liam felt his stomach knot at the words emblazoned on this screen.

Picking you up in five. Problem with Colbie.

He was dressed and standing outside the large training center behind the Prairie Winds Club with two minutes to spare when Bode's pickup slid to a stop directly in front of him ten seconds later. He hadn't even closed his door when his friend was speeding down the drive.

"Two guys stopped in the garage today, flashing a picture of Colbie to Gus and asking questions. She managed to stay hidden under your car, but she was rattled."

Liam could almost hear the 'and' in his friend's voice, so he waited for the rest of it.

"Gus said he got the impression this wasn't the first issue she's had, but for some reason, she hasn't mentioned anything to anyone."

"Let me guess—she'd managed to convince herself she was being overly cautious, maybe even paranoid." Liam had seen it before. It was human nature to tune out what the mind didn't want to accept, even when personal safety was at stake. Most of those in witness protection had already lost so much, they often had trouble facing the prospect of losing everything again. "Where is she now?"

"You aren't going to fucking believe this," Bode surprised him by laughing. "She's finishing the tune-up on your car. Evidently, you were right, she's fallen in love with that little death trap on wheels." He and Bode had very different ideas when it came to transportation. Liam preferred classic sports cars, but Bode had quickly adopted their American teammates' preference for big trucks.

The two used the outside entrance while she was working to check her small apartment for electronic monitoring devices. They'd learned a lot about her during their previous inspections. Liam hadn't missed the pictures of the Spitfire during their first walk-through and immediately started looking for one as similar as possible to the magazine photos displayed on the front of her small refrigerator.

Buying the small roadster and having it restored wasn't

cheap. But after watching Gus' security footage and seeing her reaction to what his accountant referred to as a "new line-item," he knew it had been well worth the cost. Liam rarely dipped into the trust fund his grandfather set up for him, but for once, he'd done so without apology. He'd known the time was drawing near when he and Bode would re-enter Colbie's life—he just hadn't realized it would happen today.

Chapter Two

COLBIE HAD ALMOST finished working on the Triumph when Kyle West stalked into the garage. Glancing around, she was shocked to see so many people standing nearby, but Kyle's attention was focused entirely on her. *Yippee skippy.*

She'd met Kyle and Kent the first day she'd arrived in Texas. Both men had tried to persuade her to live in one of the cottages on their property, but she'd politely declined… repeatedly. She'd known before their first meeting the Wests were well-respected, former Navy SEALs who owned their own kink club. It had taken Colbie only a few minutes in their company to know moving under their constant perusal would be a colossal mistake. She'd lived under constant scrutiny and knew too well how daunting it could be. *No thanks. Been there, done that.*

"Hi, Kyle, to what do I owe this pleasure?" It had only taken her ten minutes to finish the tune-up and the garage was already wall-to-wall testosterone, thanks to the influx of several Prairie Winds team members.

"Cute, Colbie. Very clever. I can see my brother and I made the right decision keeping you and our lovely wife apart." His words might have sounded curt, but the warmth in his eyes when he mentioned his wife gave him away.

"You're worried I'll give her tips on how to cut the

brake lines on your monster truck?" She'd quickly learned when she moved to Texas, any threat to a man's truck was taken seriously. Anytime she wanted to get under the one of the West's skin, she threatened their precious pickups.

"This is one of the reasons we wanted you living close—to keep an eye on you." When she looked up from wiping the last of the grease from her hands, he was watching her intently. Leaning back against the car, with one ankle crossed over the other, his thumbs hooked in the pockets of his dark Levi's®, he looked more like a billboard model than the owner of a wildly successful kink club.

She'd learned Kyle and his twin brother were quietly recruiting many of their government's best and brightest for their rapidly growing team of contract Special Forces operatives. Specializing in hostage rescue, the team had a passion for saving young men and women who'd unwittingly fallen into the hands of sex slave traders. She'd been told their commitment to dismantling the sex slave trade was what had brought her to their attention. When they heard what she'd done, they had volunteered to assist with her relocation.

Looking around the room, Colbie noticed everyone's attention was pointedly focused anywhere but on the two of them. *Cowards.*

"Don't you think you're overreacting a bit?" If she hadn't been watching closely, she'd have missed the muscle in his jaw tensing; it was the only outward sign he was frustrated with her. After long seconds, he shook his head.

"No, Colbie, I don't. And I'm confident this problem won't be solved by using the ostrich theory of coping." Nodding in the direction of the garage's large office, he stood to his full height and motioned her forward. "Let's chat." *Chat. Yeah, right. He's going to chat and I'm going to listen.*

KYLE WEST COULD see the defiance building in Colbie—it practically vibrated in the air around her. If he didn't talk her back from the edge, Liam and Bode were going to face a huge challenge they hadn't created. She was going to have enough trouble understanding why they'd been nearby and hadn't contacted her when she'd obviously been interested in them back in England. Dammit, this is usually Kent's specialty. *He's much better at the touchy-feely stuff than I am. The only woman I want to touch and feel-up is Tobi.*

Shaking his head at his own frustration, he tried to refocus his attention on the problem at hand rather than anticipating his sweet wife's return tonight. She and Gracie, her best friend and business partner, were flying in from Montana where they'd gone to update *a couple* of the forum shops at the Mountain Mastery Club.

Tobi and Gracie's two-day trip had mushroomed into a ten-day revamp of most of the small shops when Gracie discovered how many customers had been turned away during the previous two quarters. He smiled to himself; those two were turning out to be brilliant business women. The only downside? They were spending more and more time away from home. They needed to hire help, but so far, they hadn't found anyone they felt shared their vision and drive. The snick of the door closing broke him out of his musings.

"I'm going to cut to the chase, Colbie. The men who came into the garage today are contract mercs." He held up a hand when she would have mentioned the term could be applied to his team as well. "We don't know who's paying them—not that it would change our response. Until the slavers' network is completely dismantled, no one can know where you are."

"You don't think they'll move on?" He could hear the hope in her tone, but her expression was filled with grim acceptance. What he hadn't expected was for her to drop her gaze under his scrutiny; up to this point he'd never seen her exhibit a single submissive trait. He knew she'd been a member of The Castle Masters Club in London, but had always assumed she was a Domme.

"No, sweetness, I don't think they'll give up easily. Just as I don't believe their appearance here is a random stroke of their good luck. I also suspect there have been things which have seemed odd or unusual to you leading up to today. What I want to know is why you didn't alert someone."

"We'd be interested in hearing about that as well," Liam's deep voice filled the room as he and Bode stepped inside.

BODE SAW COLBIE'S FACE go sheet white when she saw them walk into the room. She hadn't seen them since the night they'd delivered her to headquarters, and he was certain having them walk in today of all days had seriously thrown her off balance. "Why are you here? You don't even like me." *What the fuck? Don't like her?*

Bode felt his entire body stiffen in response. Part of his reaction was from surprise, but his dick was focused on the way the soft cotton of her t-shirt molded itself to her breasts. They rose and fell in a way which assured him their heft was all natural—no silicone implants for their woman. *Their woman?* When had he laid claim to her? Sure, he wanted her. He wanted to feel her smooth skin under his hands, her peaked nipples poking into his chest. And he could hardly wait to feel her heat wrapped around his dick. But realizing he wanted more than a physical connection was a startling realization.

"Who told you that I don't like you?" The question came out harsher than he'd planned, but damn it, she'd surprised him.

"It's not like you made any effort to keep your disdain a secret. You hauled me into your headquarters like a sack of dog poo you couldn't wait to be rid of. You walked away and never looked back. I was stuck in a closet they called an interrogation room for hours... HOURS, and you never even checked on me." The longer her tirade continued, the louder it was getting. She was still running on adrenaline and had obviously decided to focus her frustration on him. Fine. He could play *bad cop* as well as anyone.

"You're wrong, but I doubt you'll listen to reason, so continue spouting off nonsense you'll regret later." He almost laughed at the murderous look on her face. She reminded him of the cartoon characters whose faces turned crimson before steam spewed out of their ears.

"Wrong? How could I possibly be wrong? Did you or did you not walk me into your super spy office and leave me? Why I expected anything different from two men who didn't say jack shit to me during the entire drive from the local police station is a mystery, but there you have it. Hell, every question I asked you was answered with a grunt. Well, guess what... I don't speak caveman. I speak English, French, and German, but when it comes to caveman, you better bring in an interpreter. Consider it a part of your accommodation budget. You know... making allowances for the less articulate, because not everyone has mastered distinguishing between polite and rude grunts. Boy, oh boy. You take the cake and the custard, too. I don't think you said ten words to me after you interrogated me."

When he frowned, she shook her head and held her hand up. "Don't even try to deny that was an interrogation. Rapid fire questions, one after the other, equals interrogation. Look it up. You were polite and attentive, even flirty until you juiced the last drop of information from me. Damn, I felt like an orange or something. Squeezed until the last drop was gone, then you tossed me aside like a piece of garbage. Not great for my ego. Don't know why I was hur...surprised. Happens all the time. As soon as guys find out I know more about their cars than they do, they're gone."

A bolt of pain lanced his chest at her near slip of the tongue. Knowing she'd been hurt by their actions didn't sit well with him. She was pacing the length of the office, arms flailing in the air, boots slapping the concrete floor so loudly, he wondered if her teeth were clattering with each step. When it didn't seem as though she was going to wind down, he looked at Kyle, who appeared to be struggling to hold back his laughter.

"That's enough." His sharp tone brought her to an immediate stop. "You've made so many inaccurate statements, I'm not sure where to start. First of all, we did not interrogate you. We asked the questions we needed answered because we wanted to take apart the criminal enterprise you inadvertently stumbled in to. You have no idea how long we'd waited for a break in that case. Hell, you were the answer to our prayers." *In more ways than I'm prepared to admit.*

"It's true, little Spitfire. Every answer you gave was

invaluable in the investigation. We were able to rescue twenty-three people because of your quick thinking." Liam's soft tone and soothing words had the desired effect. Bode watched some of the tension drain from her slender shoulders.

"And as for not chatting you up during the drive, you should know it was draining all my energy to focus on the road when all I wanted to do was peel those oil-stained overalls from you and find out what delectable treats were hidden underneath all that bravado. Hell, it's a miracle you made it out of the parking lot with a stitch of clothing on. I couldn't have carried on a conversation to save my life. For the love of all things holy, woman, my oxygen deprived brain was barely functioning enough to drive because the majority of my blood was in my dick."

Colbie's mouth gaped open in shock. Bode assumed his blunt words had offended the petite blue-blood, so he was astonished by her reply.

"You got a hard-on because of me?"

"See?" Liam snorted a laugh that defied his own upper-class background. "I told you she was bright."

"Oh, yeah, there's no slipping anything past NASA's newest recruit. Now, if the three of you can table this part of the discussion until later, I'd like to move things along. My wife will be home in a couple of hours, and I want to be home waiting when she arrives. My brother and I plan to let her spend some time with the kids before they head to our parents' house for the weekend."

The heat in Kyle's eyes was impossible to miss. The man loved his job, he was passionate about the work the Prairie Winds team did. Kyle was also committed to the kink club he and his brother founded. The club had quickly become one of the most popular and well-respected in the country. Their focus on the safety and privacy of their members had become almost as legendary as the stories of their heroism as Navy SEALs. It spoke volumes about their leadership that so many of the men who'd served with and under them joined the team when they left military service. But it was Kyle's utter devotion to his wife that burned in his eyes now.

Watching Kyle and Kent interact with their spirited little sub had been both entertaining and educational. Tobi West could only be described as a force of nature. She was whip-smart and as full of sass as any woman Bode had ever met. She was also loyal to her friends and had a heart as big as the state she called home. When the Wests moved into the new home they'd built on the Prairie Winds compound, Liam and Bode moved into their penthouse apartment above the club. Tobi seemed to adopt them after that and over the past several months they'd started to consider her the little sister neither of them had.

Bode and Liam hadn't hesitated when Kent and Kyle first approached them. Working for MI6 brought with it all the challenges of having the government breathing down your neck. The limits made it almost impossible to be effective, and they'd both been on the fast track to burning out before their thirty-fifth birthdays. Bode had always envisioned the two of them sharing a wife, but he'd known their family connections in the UK would have made the arrangement impossible.

"I'm going to cut to the chase, Colbie. You can't stay here. It's far too dangerous and until we get this all sorted out, you'll be staying at Prairie Winds. There isn't an open cottage right now, so you'll stay in the apartment above the club. It's got plenty of room for the three of you. Let's go. I'll send someone upstairs to pack up your things. Your safety is our primary concern."

Bode watched Colbie's eyes widen as Kyle steamrolled her. He knew what was coming, he could see the battle brewing in her bright blue eyes.

Wait for it… three, two, one.

Chapter Three

COLBIE WAS SO pissed, she was sure the top of her head was going to blow like one of the exploding manhole covers she'd seen on YouTube. Kyle West might be horny as hell and anxious to get home, so he could fuck Tobi blind, but that wasn't her problem. And it certainly didn't give him any right to play God in her life.

"Hold up, Kyle. I agree those guys represent a problem, but that doesn't give you the right to waltz in here big as you please and start ordering me around. Holy Christmas and Blessed Easter, who died and left you king, anyway?" He looked like he'd just sucked on a lemon, and she was sure she'd heard him growl. Liam on the other hand looked mildly amused while Bode was glaring at her like she was an errant child.

Kent West stepped into the room, his gaze moving from his brother to her and then moving to the other two men standing to the side. He shook his head and sighed.

"Fucking hell, I'm sorry, Colbie. I was hoping to get here before Kyle pissed you off. He has all the finesse of a runaway Mack truck."

"I've simply explained the facts. She's being unreasonable. I think we should do a DNA test, she and Tobi must be related. It's probably distant, but there are too many similarities to be coincidental."

"Thank you, Kyle. That's the nicest thing anyone's said

to me in a long time." Colbie hoped her fake sweet tone gave him a cavity or two. *Asshat.*

"Not helpful, little spitfire." Liam's quiet admonishment made her feel about two inches tall. She understood Kyle was just trying to help, but she was damned tired of people deciding what was best for her and then issuing edicts she was expected to follow. "Take a deep breath." She did so before she realized she'd just followed another order. Her inner child stomped her foot in frustration. *Dammit.* Liam stepped in front of her and tipped her chin up with his fingers until she met his gaze.

"Are you arguing because you think Kyle is wrong? Or are you reacting to the way the information was presented?"

Damn and double damn. She'd hoped no one would make that connection, but she shouldn't have expected any grace when she was standing in a room full of Dominants. Closing her eyes, Colbie tried to hold back her frustration and the tears that usually accompanied it. It was a vicious cycle... frustration led to tears which amped up her frustration even more, making her cry harder. Biting the inside of her cheeks to hold back the tidal wave of emotion, Colbie almost screamed when she felt strong hands grip her upper arms.

"Look at me, Colbie." When she opened her eyes, Liam's face swam in her vision. "I know you're overwhelmed. You've spent months settling in and now if feels like it's all slipping away."

She hadn't realized how worried she'd been the past couple of weeks. The small signs she'd found had become increasingly difficult to ignore, and she hadn't slept more than a couple of hours each night for the past week. Colbie felt herself sway as fatigue and the heavy weight of emotion finally started to pull her under. By the time her knees buckled, her vision was already dimming, and the voices around her sounded like they were coming from the other end of a tunnel. It wasn't worth the effort to fight the darkness, so she let herself slid into the peaceful silence.

LIAM WAS GLAD HE'D already had his hands on her because Colbie had dropped like a stone. He'd watched her eyes glaze with exhaustion and wondered when she'd last slept, a split second before she went completely limp. Scooping her up into his arms, he headed directly out the door. There was no reason to stand around chitchatting. He was grateful the other members of the team had moved Bode's pickup inside the garage, making it easy to settle her on the backseat. The garage was close to Prairie Winds, so she wouldn't need to stay out of sight long; and carrying her from the building was sure to catch the interest of anyone watching.

"She's beginning to come around. Make sure she stays down until you're clear. I'll be right behind you." Liam slammed the pickup door and backed his car out of the bay. No one would think anything of them leaving separately; the men looking for Colbie would have seen his car when they'd been in the garage earlier. When they parked in the secured garage beneath the club a few minutes later, his shoulders sagged in relief.

Colbie's eyes went wide in surprise when she saw him getting out of his car. "Oh my God. That's your car?" A myriad of emotions reflected in her eyes in a flash so quick it reminded him of the child's game of thumbing a stack of still pictures to make the individual shots appear to move.

"It's my dream car. I even have pictures on..." He saw her eyes narrow as her quick mind started fitting pieces into the puzzle.

He had no intention of having this discussion in the garage. Although they weren't completely exposed, their conversation could certainly be overheard by the men monitoring the security feeds. "Let's discuss this inside." Grasping her elbow, he moved her toward the door as Bode tapped in the code. Micah Drake, the West's computer and security guru, had a sweet setup, and the man's contacts were the stuff of legend. Colbie might envy his car, but Liam envied Micah's technology.

"We'll get you a keycard for the door and elevator later. For now, you won't need them." Bode was flanking Colbie's other side. They had her sandwiched between them, and he smiled at her quick intake of breath when she realized they were standing much closer than would ordinarily be considered polite. When she shifted to step away, Bode's low voice filled the small space. "Don't move. You will stay where we put you, Storeen." Liam smiled to himself. If Bode was calling her his little treasure, his friend was as smitten with Colbie as Liam was. The only time the poetic influences of ancient Gaelic peppered Bode's speech was when emotion was coloring his usually measured words.

When the elevator doors opened, Colbie whistled. "Holy shit, Sherlocks." Liam leaned his head back and laughed at her obvious pun about their former occupation. They hadn't work for Scotland Yard, but most people didn't know enough about the United Kingdom's answer to the CIA to joke about it. "This is incredible. It reminds me of the manager's quarters at The Castle Masters Club in London."

Liam had read her file until he had the damned thing committed to memory, so her mention of the exclusive BDSM club wasn't a complete surprise. But hearing that she'd been in the manager's private apartment set him back.

"Why were you in Master Deacon's apartment, Spitfire?"

Colbie didn't answer for long seconds. Instead, she appeared to be enthralled with the décor of the penthouse. Her fascination surprised him, considering she hadn't done any decorating in the small apartment over the garage. If fact, he doubted it would have taken her more than five minutes to shove everything in a bag and be out the door. Her *go bag* was well stocked and stashed under the floorboards beneath the bed. If he hadn't known what to look for, he'd have missed the small, hidden niche.

"I've been to a lot of parties in that apartment. I always receive a personal invitation from Master Deacon." Her response sent a lightning bolt of unexpected jealousy through him and from the murderous look on Bode's face, he wasn't faring any better. She shook her head and smiled. "You two are so easy. Deacon is my Godfather."

He blinked at her as if that would clear his confusion. "Godfather? Why isn't that in your file?" It was almost impossible to believe that detail would have escaped them. And if they'd missed something that significant, what else had they missed?

"I don't know why it would be. It's not like it's something anyone needs to know." Wrong. It was exactly the sort of thing they needed to know. After they'd left the agency, word of her membership to the posh kink club filtered out to them, but no one mentioned her personal association with Deacon Campbell. "Deacon let me join the club, but he didn't let me have any fun."

"Define fun." Liam didn't realize he was clenching his fists at his sides until she looked down and paled. When she started to take a step back, Liam forced his fingers to relax and took a deep breath before speaking again. "Neither of us would ever hurt you, Colbie."

"Well, not in anger, anyway. That's not to say I'm not itching to see what shade of pink my hand print will turn on your pert little ass." Bode's words were barely audible, but when Colbie's cheeks turned scarlet, Liam knew she hadn't missed the comment.

"Deacon was very protective. He wouldn't let me go into the lower dungeon levels. He let me take the training classes for submissives, and a couple of the dungeon masters used me for demos, but that was it. The one time I tried to negotiate a scene with a Dom, Deacon scared the guy off." When Liam and Bode both grinned, she rolled her eyes. "It was embarrassing."

Ordinarily, having a woman roll her eyes at him was grounds for an immediate paddling, but Liam held his tongue. After all, Colbie had only been in their care less than an hour. His gut told him she was a natural sub, and evidently, Deacon thought so as well. But until they'd had a chance to get her settled and at least discuss the basics, his palm wouldn't be going anywhere near her bare ass.

"Being under Master Deacon's perusal should have made you feel safe rather than uncomfortable." Bode's words earned him a glare, making his eyes narrow, meeting her frown with one of his own. "Glaring at a Dom is never a good idea, Pet. It's universally understood to be an invitation for punishment. You glare at a Dom downstairs, and you'll find yourself bent over the nearest horizontal surface, bare ass to the wind before you've taken a deep breath."

When she opened her mouth to protest, Liam's raised brow stilled the words before they spilled out. The protest he'd seen dancing on the tip of her tongue might have seemed more convincing if her breathing hadn't quickened and her eyes dilated at Bode's warning. Liam decided it was time to steer the conversation in a different direction.

"When was the last time you ate, Colbie?" He knew from their frequent forays into her apartment there was never much food available. Hell, there had been times he wondered if she ever cooked anything other than eggs and grilled cheese sandwiches.

COLBIE HAD JUST opened her mouth to answer Liam's inquiry when the elevator door opened and Kent West stepped into the room. "Sorry to barge in, but these were left downstairs along with a warning from my brother." When she noticed her bags in his hand, Colbie had a sinking feeling about the warning. "It seems Tobi has some competition when it comes to a complete lack of cooking expertise." His face broke out in a huge grin that made him look more like a mischievous teenager than a former Navy SEAL turned kink club owner.

"My warning is for the two of you." He pointed at Liam and Bode, but he never took his eyes off her. "She is not allowed to cook. Period. Nothing. We are just now getting back in the good graces of the local fire department and neither Kyle nor I want to start the process over again." He grinned again and tilted his head to the side as if considering how to ask the question she knew was coming.

"Care to tell me what the stench was in your apartment, Colbie? Kyle compared it to the rotten egg gas we made in high school chemistry. That shit was so rank they canceled classes for the rest of the day. As I recall, our parents were none too amused when the principal called them." She knew Kent had used his own story to soften his question, but she could also see his determination. There wasn't a chance on Earth she'd be able to avoid answering.

"Eggs. I usually just scrambled them. I found a video on-line that made it look pretty easy and it was. But then my little microwave bit the dust, and I looked up how to make soft boiled eggs. The cook at my parents always made them for me, and I didn't realize you had to watch the clock so carefully."

Shuffling her booted feet, she suddenly felt very out of place. Her grease stained clothing made her look like a street urchin, and the three men standing in front of her all looked like they'd just stepped out of a fashion magazine. Even Kent West's jeans were crisply pressed, and his oxford shirt was so white, it probably glowed in the dark.

"Did you know egg shells will burn to the bottom of a pan? Well, they do… right before they explode. The video didn't mention anything about that happening. Or the stench."

"How long did you leave them unattended, Storeen?"

"I don't know for sure. I sort of forgot about them and went out for a run." Running wasn't her favorite exercise, but since she didn't have access to a lap pool, it was the only way she had to expend all the pent-up stress. "When I got back, a guy walking by on the sidewalk in front of the garage told me he thought he'd heard a gunshot. He was going to call the police, but I talked him out of it." She looked from Liam's menacing expression to Bode who looked like his head was going to explode before she heard

Kent's snort of laughter.

"You two have your work cut out for you. I could give you some pointers, but I think it'll be more fun to stand back and watch you figure it out on your own. I can't begin to tell you what a fucking déjà vu moment this is. And I can tell by the looks on your faces, you're trying to decide which is worse, the fire hazard, talking a stranger out of calling for help, or returning alone to her apartment."

"Why wouldn't I go back in? I remembered the eggs as soon as I rounded the corner and headed down the ally. And I've met most of the local police and darned well didn't want them razzing me about overcooking a couple eggs."

"I know from experience it takes more than a couple of eggs to smell bad enough to elicit that response from Kyle. He wouldn't even go home to shower—said he didn't want to take the smell into our house." Kent burst out laughing and it took almost a full minute for him to calm down enough to continue. "You can't believe the shit we've seen over the years. We were deployed in some of the nastiest hell holes on the planet, and he swears he's never smelled anything like that."

Colbie couldn't hold back her grin because it was obvious he was deliberately exaggerating the story Kyle had probably already spun like fine gold thread. Leveling a look at her, he pointed his finger and all hint of humor evaporated like a summer shower on the hot Texas turf. "As for running into a space when someone tells you they've heard gunfire, sweetness, that shit stops now. That expression about fools rushing in where angels fear to tread? Don't be a fool, because if angels are worried, you should be too."

Chapter Four

BODE WATCHED AS the elevator doors slid closed as Kent West gave them both sympathetic looks. *Asshole.* Shaking his head, Bode heard Liam ask Colbie again about when she'd last eaten.

"I had some yogurt for lunch." She'd spent so much time cleaning up the mess in her apartment last night, she hadn't eaten any dinner, and the place still smelled so bad this morning, she hadn't wanted to stick around long enough to eat breakfast. She'd grabbed the small carton of yogurt and bolted out the door as quickly as possible.

The litany of curses from both men made her cringe. They directed her to the kitchen and after ordering her to stay seated at the largest marble-topped island she'd ever seen, the two of them got to work. Their movements were so seamless, they looked like they'd been choreographed. Neither of them wasted any effort; every step was purposeful and they never seemed to be in the other's way. In no time at all, they'd assembled a large pan of lasagna which was now baking and a salad which Bode put in the fridge to chill. It wasn't until both men turned to her that she realized she'd been staring at them. Liam grinned, and she felt her face flush.

"Like what you see, Spitfire?"

Colbie felt the flush move up her face in a wave of searing heat. There wasn't any reason to deny her obvious appreciation, but she didn't see any reason to feed their egos by answering, either. So, she didn't respond. His smile dimmed as he crossed his arms over his chest.

"I expect you to answer when I ask you a question, Colbie. Not only is it the polite thing to do, it's also something every Dom at the Prairie Winds Club will expect of you."

"You might want to review Master Deacon's training manual. I'm fairly certain this would have been covered." She'd have been offended by Bode's tone if she hadn't seen the heat blazing in his eyes. For a few seconds, she allowed relief to wash over her. Knowing they were attracted to her despite her appearance was empowering.

"What are you thinking, Spitfire?"

Colbie had spent enough time with Deacon when he was in Master-mode to recognize Liam's tone. That wasn't a simple question, it was a command for information. "I was just relieved that you don't seem to mind how I look. I mean, I'm probably not your usual type, so…" she didn't get the chance to finish the thought before both men started moving around the kitchen island.

"Not our usual *type*? What's our usual type, Spitfire?"

There was no way to answer Liam's question without digging herself deeper into the hole she found herself in. Never one to shy away from a confrontation, Colbie blurted out what she'd pictured as their usual type.

"Tall and gorgeous. Not a hair out of place. Perfect nails and dressed to kill. A woman who hangs on your every word." *And spends more time on her knees than on her feet when you're around.*

She saw the muscles of his jaw tighten as he bit out, "How very open minded of you, *dear*." *Then why did that endearment sound more menacing than sweet?* Something close to hurt flashed in his eyes, and for a few seconds, she felt guilty. Perhaps her assessment of them as shallow had been harsh, but she'd done her research and knew how accurate it had been. She'd accurately described every woman they'd been photographed with at social and charity events over the past decade.

"No man worth having wants a woman with grease under her fingernails, Guinevere." Her mother's voice floated through her mind, but she quickly pushed aside the pain those memories brought. It wasn't safe for the past to intrude on her present. Mistakes could easily cost her the little sliver of stability she'd found in Texas.

The one thing she'd worried most about was being forced to move. She enjoyed her job, and she knew she could find a new one if she had to, but the security she felt knowing the Prairie Winds Team was nearby would be impossible to replace. Even though she'd decided against living in one of their cottages, she'd taken a lot of comfort knowing they were just minutes away.

Colbie had learned how quickly everything she valued could be stolen from her. She didn't regret going to the authorities with the information she'd overheard, but she also understood too well what it had cost her. Seeing the news of the young women and men being returned to their families was satisfying, but the whole mess had turned her world upside down.

The first few weeks she'd been in witness protection had been the worst. Forced to stay hidden inside one of MI6's safe houses had nearly driven her insane. When she'd learned Kent and Kyle West had offered their assistance, she'd been both elated and terrified. She'd visited the United States several times, but she'd never lived anywhere except London.

Everything she'd known about Texas, she'd learned from the movies, and it hadn't taken her long to find out how uninformed she was. Her narrow view had expanded exponentially in the past year, and she'd come to love her adopted home. The vast state, three times larger than the UK, had such a varied topography, it was fun to explore. Colbie had spent every weekend for months traveling and swore she'd never seen the same thing twice.

"I'm not sure I've ever seen anyone drift away so easily."

"It's remarkable. I'm starting to understand the Wests' concern for Tobi's safety when she floats in and out of awareness." The two of them might have been teasing, but she knew there was a lot of truth in their words.

"I guess this means I feel safe with the two of you." *Though I'm not sure why.*

"Good save, Spitfire." She gave him a cheesy grin, but didn't think he'd been fooled by her attempt to redeem herself. There wasn't any reason to deny her earlier lack of focus; she was cognizant enough to know how dangerous inattention could be. The stories she'd been told by the agents in charge of settling her in to the program had been terrifying. She had no desire to become one of their statistics.

"What the hell are you thinking about? You just went deathly pale." Bode was suddenly standing right in front of her, his fingers tilting her chin up until their eyes met.

Taking a deep breath, this time she hesitated to answer. There was such a thing as too much personal information when she had no idea where they stood. *As far as I know, they're just babysitting. Don't assume a man is interested just because he smiles at you, Guinevere. How many times did I hear my mother say that? And for fuck's sake, stop talking to yourself.*

Liam burst out laughing beside her and when she refocused on Bode, amusement lit his chocolate colored eyes. "We are not in any way interested in babysitting you. I'm not even going to start on all the reasons that's inaccurate. Our interest in you started the minute you hit our radar, Storeen."

Realizing she'd said the words aloud should have embarrassed her, but she pushed those feelings aside, she'd already made herself look like a ninny.

"What does that mean? I know I've heard that word before, but I can't remember where."

"Probably English Lit in college. It's ancient Gaelic. Bode slips into it on the rare occasions his thinking veers from logic to emotion." She could hear the amusement in Liam's voice and to her surprise, Bode's cheeks pinked ever so slightly.

"It means little treasure."

She felt herself relax. If he was referring to her as a treasure, perhaps they weren't just guarding her until she could be relocated.

"I really appreciate your habit of speaking your thoughts aloud. It's a huge help to know what all those fleeting expressions mean."

Colbie had never considered herself a pushover, but she could sense how easily these two could steamroll her. They wouldn't do it with force. Their coercion would be wrapped in beautiful paper and tied with a shiny satin bow. Deciding she needed a few minutes out of their realm of influence, she took a small step back and straightened her spine.

"I need to take a shower before dinner. Can you show me to your guest room?"

Liam's eyes narrowed almost imperceptibly, but she didn't miss the shift. "I'll show you to the room you'll be using." Something in his tone sounded... odd, but she shrugged and followed him down the hall. When she started to grab her bags, Bode shook his head and scooped them up, carrying them effortlessly down the hall. They passed several closed doors and she was beginning to wonder how many bedrooms the apartment could possibly have. As if reading her mind, Liam looked back over his shoulder and gave her a tight smile. "We'll give you the nickel tour later. There are bedrooms, closets, and an office down this hall. The playroom and another large bathroom are on the other side of the living room."

"A playroom? You don't go to the club downstairs?"

"Kyle and Kent said they often played up here to avoid being interrupted with club business. And they didn't like playing in public during Tobi's pregnancy because they knew how self-conscious she was."

"She's very petite. I'll bet carrying twins made her feel as round as she was tall." She'd heard Tobi make that remark, but Colbie didn't want to risk getting the other woman in trouble by revealing that. Tobi had also mentioned how frustrated her husbands got if she made disparaging remarks about herself. Colbie didn't know the other woman well, but they'd chatted when Tobi brought her large SUV into the garage for repairs.

"Wait. Is this the master bedroom?" She wasn't entirely sure why she'd bothered to ask because it was so obviously a master suite. The room was enormous with a triple-tiered ceiling with embossed tin lining the peak. Hidden track lighting along the tiers made the ceiling glow and the effect was spectacular. "This is amazing. I've never seen a ceiling like this."

The bed was on a pedestal, making it the focal point of the room. The coverlet looked more like a feather tick with various blue and purple swirls that looked like a cross between Monet's and Van Gogh's starry night paintings.

"Yes, it's the master. The bath is through that door and the closet is here." Liam opened the door to a closet which was larger than the one in her parents' home in London. She watched Bode set her bags on the padded bench in the center of the closet. Her mouth dropped open when he began unpacking her things. It wasn't until that moment she wondered which one of the men from the Prairie Wind team had been tasked with packing for her. Thinking about someone touching her lingerie sent a wave of heat from her chest to her cheeks. "Do you see how much he is enjoying touching your pretty panties, Spitfire? I can assure you he'll relish tearing them off you even more."

She gasped, but didn't respond.

"Personally, I think they are a waste of money, and I'll prefer you go without, so I can run my fingers through the wet folds of your pussy and push you to the brink, no matter where we are. It will be fun to see if you can hold back your scream when you come during our first dinner party." Liam was pressed against her back with one arm banded over her upper torso with his hand cupping the opposite shoulder. *When did he move?*

"Your heart is racing and your breathing just shifted, Spitfire. I think you like hearing my plans for you. And if mine elicit this response, I can't wait to see how you react when you hear what Bode has up his sleeve."

Her imagination kicked into high gear, and the lecherous grin on Bode's face was tantamount to throwing gas on a fire. Desire spiraled from her core up her spine, then streaked back down to her sex like a bolt of lightning. Her skin started to tingle and everything around her dimmed.

"Breathe, Colbie." Liam's command was whispered against the sensitive shell of her ear before he bit down hard enough to startle her. She shuddered and sucked in several gulping breaths. When her vision cleared, Colbie found Bode standing directly in front of her.

"That's something we're going to work on, sweetness. We're not into breath play. Gasping and screaming are perfectly acceptable, however." The grin was back but this time it was accompanied by the molten look of pure, unveiled lust in his eyes.

Liam turned her and gave her ass a firm swat. "Take your shower and then we'll eat. We'll leave clothing for you on the bed. Wear it. Nothing more. Nothing less." *Right. Like less would be an option.* Even the more moderate areas of the club Deacon had allowed her in had taught her a lot about the *clothing optional* concept touted on the Castle Masters website. She'd seen how little regard Doms had for clothing. They also seemed to be more than happy to relieve their subs of pieces if they offered any protest about what they were given to wear.

"Yes, Sir." Her response had been automatic and when Bode arched his brow, she felt herself flush. "I watched Deacon take a piece of clothing from one of the subs in my training class every time she commented or frowned about the outfit he'd given her to wear. As you can imagine, in no time at all, she was completely naked."

"I'm glad you learned from her mistake. And don't worry, since we're eating lasagna, you'll be reasonably covered. Neither of us wants to see you burned by hot sauce or pasta."

"Thank you. I promise I won't be long." Stepping into the master bath was like walking into a magazine layout of the perfect personal spa. The bathtub looked more like a small pool, and she had a sudden flash of how much smaller it would seem if she was sandwiched between Liam and Bode. Both men were well over six-foot-tall, and their broad shoulders would quickly fill the space. Shaking off the vision of their naked bodies glistening with water as she slid between them, Colbie quickly stripped out of her clothes and stepped into the shower.

Geez. Get a grip and live in the moment because it's entirely likely that's all you'll have.

Chapter Five

"THE ONLY THINGS in here worth saving are her panties and bras." Bode surveyed the contents of Colbie's clothing bag and shuddered. "Hell, even her work out clothes are little more than rags. Why the hell isn't she using her trust fund money?" MI6 had convinced her parents to donate Colbie's trust fund to fighting the sex trade and then immediately set it up in an account for her. The money laundering had been nothing short of genius, and the only person who'd been worried about it being traced back to her was Colbie.

"You know perfectly well why she isn't using it." Liam's even tone was irritating simply because Bode knew he was right.

"I swear I'm going to take her shopping, then burn these in the middle of the damned driveway, just to make a statement." He would, too. She was a beautiful woman who'd been thrust into a world she was ill-prepared for. In the process, she'd forgotten to nurture her feminine side. Bode didn't intend to deny her the joy she found in working on motors, but he planned to show her the joy of embracing more than one side of her personality. Storming out of the room, he cast a glance over his shoulder.

"Check the food and I'll get her one of my shirts, and then, I'm pulling everything back out of the closet and washing it. The smoke smell alone might set of the alarms." He heard Liam's snort of laughter as he stalked to his own room. He and his friend had each claimed a guest bedroom after the remodel, hoping that sometime soon they'd have Colbie between them in the master suite.

Returning a few seconds later, Bode started tossing her clothing into a small basket. He smiled when he heard her singing softly in the shower. He was surprised she'd left the bathroom door open; he wasn't about to let the opportunity to observe her slip through his fingers. Her slender form was silhouetted in the steam-covered glass, but it wasn't difficult for his imagination to fill in the blanks. Unconsciously rubbing his palms down the legs of his slacks, Bode's palms were itching in anticipation.

Damn, he wished he could step inside to watch her hands sliding over her breasts. He'd encourage her to enjoy the sensuous feeling of her fingers pinching and pulling those tight nipples until they were drawn up into tight points. As her Dom that pleasure would belong to him—it would be his to share as he saw fit. But they weren't there yet. Pushing himself away from the doorframe, he smiled when he recognized the song. *Yes, sweetheart, if you say I have a beautiful body, I'll definitely hold it against you.* He draped his shirt over the foot of the bed, picked up the basket of stench-covered clothing, and sauntered out of the room, grinning ear to ear as anticipation thrummed through his body.

When he reentered kitchen, Liam's eyes were glowing with the same eagerness Bode felt. "She's going to be ours. I can feel it."

"We'll see. I hope so, but I'm trying to not get too far ahead of myself. I don't think this is will be an easy transition for her. She isn't going to open herself up easily. The program trainers did a great job of teaching her the importance of distance." Bode understood the importance of the training she'd been given, but it was going to make reaching her on an emotional level more difficult.

"It won't be easy, but nothing worthwhile ever is. We need to gain her trust. Remember, she thinks she is only here for her protection."

"Which is bullshit since we've been plotting for months how to bring her into our lives." This was the first time since he'd moved to the U.S. he felt things were finally beginning to fall in place. For the first few months, they'd been busy moving and training, so they'd been forced to stand by and let others watch over Colbie. It had been frustrating and hadn't brought out the best in either of them. By the time they'd finished their training, he'd considered it a small miracle they hadn't been fired. It wasn't as if either of them needed the money—it was the principle of the thing, not to mention the satisfaction they found in making the world a safer place.

Bode felt her before he turned to find Colbie hesitantly stepping into the room. Her cheeks were still flushed from her shower, and her hair stuck up like red spikes. She looked more like a sprite than a full-grown woman. She'd obviously put on the shirt while still damp because portions of the fine cotton were nearly transparent. Hell, he might insist she always dress exactly like this every evening for dinner. Without saying anything, Bode held out his hand and was pleased when she walked to him without hesitation.

"You are temptation personified, Storeen. I know we said we would eat before discussing things, but I want to hear you say you're interested." He'd been intentionally vague. For now, he'd let her make her own interpretation. They could work out the details after they'd eaten, but his raging hunger for her needed to be addressed before they sat down to share a meal.

"Yes. I mean, yes, I'm interested in spending time with you, even if I don't know exactly what you're expecting. The biggest lesson I've learned is how quickly things can change. One moment in time can change the entire direction of your life. Everything you hold dear can be taken away from you in the blink of an eye, so it's important to live in the moment."

It troubled him to hear the sadness underlying her words. It was true—stepping into the police station that night had changed Colbie's life in a lot of ways and so far, very few of those had been for the better. He knew she didn't regret the decision, but that didn't mean she didn't miss her family and friends. If they were going to convince her they were serious, they'd need to fulfill her emotional needs as well as the physical. Helping her make friends would go a long way to make her feel more settled.

"That's all we need right now, Spitfire. Let's eat before it gets cold. The sooner we eat, the sooner we can talk."

And the sooner we can get our hands on you. Liam might not have said the words out loud, but Bode knew his friend almost as well as he knew himself.

LIAM WATCHED THE INTERPLAY between Bode and Colbie, pleased at how quickly his friend was assuming the role of her Dom. For a man who'd just said he was going to hold back, Bode seemed to be rolling full steam ahead. When Liam had turned from the stove to see Colbie standing in the doorway, he'd been completely thunderstruck. Red spiked hair pointing haphazardly in every direction, freshly scrubbed face glowing from what had obviously been a long, hot shower, and the almost transparent shirt Bode had given her, combined to make Colbie the most beautiful woman he'd ever seen.

The red was too stark for her ivory skin tone, and he looked forward to seeing her natural blonde hair again. He'd talk to Tobi and arrange for a girls' spa day. He was sure their little Spitfire expected to return to work, but that wasn't going to happen. Kent was arranging for her to work part-time with the caretaker of the compound. Don Reynolds would be thrilled to have her help since he was currently overwhelmed with the number of projects Tobi managed to talk her husbands into.

Don and his wife, Patty, had been the previous owners of the property. When their vacation ranch business began to fold, they'd sold the large estate to the Wests and agreed to stay on as caretakers. Theirs was the largest cabin on the property, and they were also members of the club. Tobi swore there wasn't anything Don couldn't fix and Patty accused her of inflating his ego. Liam admired the friendship the five of them had forged. Kent had told him remodeling the property had taken a full year, but he swore it had been worth every headache and challenge they'd encountered.

Working in the on-site garage would give Colbie something to keep her mind busy while they tracked down and dealt with whoever had managed to find her. The slave ring had been furious with the raid which cost them several million dollars. They'd vowed to make an example of the woman who'd dared to cross them. It was Liam and Bode's job to make sure that didn't happen.

Settling her between them at the bar, Liam tapped the inside of her knee. "Part of being interested means you'll be exposed to new things, and one of those is being accessible." She moved her legs apart just far enough for him to slide his hand between her thighs. Bode did the same, and they pulled outward until her knees were spread wide enough. "Hook your feet around the legs of your chair. Perfect. Now, keep your legs open, Spitfire, I assure you it will be worth the effort."

Ordinarily, he'd place a towel on the chair and have her lift the shirt so she was even more exposed. But he'd intentionally left the shirt under her, knowing any trace of wetness from arousal would be easy to see when she stood. It might make him seem like a caveman, but he was looking forward to seeing the evidence of her desire. Knowing he could elicit a physical response from a woman was satisfying, but when that woman was Colbie, it was a fucking rush.

They ate in companionable silence, but midway through the meal, he felt her stiffen beside him. Suppressing his smile, Liam looked down to see Bode's hand stroking the inside of Colbie's thigh. Her fork was suspended in the air, halfway between her plate and her mouth, as a full-body shudder moved through her. The flush, which had faded from her cheeks while they ate, returned in a heated rush. *Perfect.*

"What's Bode doing to you, Spitfire?" Without moving her fork, she turned to him, eyes wide and pupils dilating quickly. He loved that look. She might have taken the submissive training class in London, but she didn't have any practical experience. It was going to be a joy to set the submissive in her free. "I asked you a question, Colbie, and I expect an answer."

She took a deep breath as she visibly tried to push back against her growing arousal. With practice, it would be easier for her to focus while her body screamed for release. But right now, her brain was fogged to the point she couldn't do more than blink at him like a deer caught in headlights.

Liam knew when Bode stilled his movements by the slight sagging of her shoulders. He knew the relief was a double-edged sword. A part of her regretted the loss of Bode's touch, but the good girl in her knew she needed to answer his question. "His hand was... well, his fingers were... fuck-a-dilly circus."

Without giving her a chance to finish, Liam turned her until she faced him. "Try again, Spitfire, and this time, without the foul language. You'll earn yourself a lot of time over our laps if you don't exorcise profanity from your speech." Surprise and rebellion followed one another quickly in her eyes before he saw reluctant acceptance take their place.

"That must be a Dom thing. I've heard Tobi say her husbands get all bent out of shape about her language. Not that it seems to have made much difference to hear Gracie tell it. And Deacon always went off the deep end about cursing, too. What is that about anyway? Is it in the Dom handbook or something? Some sort of Universal Dominant Commandment? Holy hell....o, I should probably just not talk. I haven't had to be a prissy debutante in a long time, and let's face it, I never was any good at it, anyway." Aside from her interrogation, this was the most he'd ever heard her say. When he glanced at Bode, he could see the other man was as surprised and amused as he was.

Liam couldn't hold in his laughter any longer. "I promise we aren't trying to turn you into a *prissy debutant*. What we want from you isn't anything close to propriety. Foul language isn't particularly becoming for anyone."

"We won't care if you use fuck in the proper context." Bode grinned when she blinked her eyes in confusion. "For example, 'Master, would you fuck me, please?' would be perfectly acceptable."

Liam was relieved to hear her giggle. The tinkling sound of joy was the sweetest sound he'd ever heard.

"I see. So, if it benefits you, then it's okay?"

"Yes," Bode agreed, "I'd say that about covers it."

Chapter Six

COLBIE WAS GOING batshit crazy. The caretaker and his wife were out of town, so she hadn't been able to start working in the garage. Liam and Bode had stopped discussing her return to Gus' after she'd hounded them for three hours. And her attempt to circumvent them by pleading her cause to Kent West had proven to be a huge mistake. It turns out their claim to not be full-time Doms wasn't entirely accurate.

After their talk last night, they'd refused to let her make a decision about exploring the lifestyle until she'd slept on it... alone. She didn't know about them, but she hadn't gotten much sleep after their discussion. Who could possibly sleep after discussing all manners of kink with two men so hot, she wondered if they'd burn her fingers? And she wasn't ashamed to admit getting herself off had been more than a passing thought. But when she'd dug around in her bag, she'd discovered every single one of her toys missing. Bode had returned her freshly laundered clothing while she was rifling through the smallest bag. She hadn't noticed him leaning against the doorframe until he chuckled.

"Problems?" When she growled in frustration, he set the basket aside and moved to stand in front of her. "If you're looking for your toys, you aren't going to find them."

"I told you she'd be looking for those. It's never good to wind up a sub and then leave them to their own devices. They tend to take matters in their own hands—literally." Liam's amused voice sounded from behind her. She turned and looked behind him, wondering how he'd gotten into the room without her seeing him enter. "There's a second exit. You didn't think Kent and Kyle would leave their most precious possession without a second means of escape, do you?"

"To be honest, I hadn't had time to think about it, but I did wonder why neither of you used this room." Bode was surprised the question hadn't come up during their earlier conversation.

"We've been waiting for you, Storeen." Bode knew his words surprised her, but sometimes the truth is very simple.

"We are looking forward to sharing this room with you, Spitfire, but we are men of our word, and despite the fact I'm fucking dying to get my hands on you, it's not happening tonight. We want you to think about what we'll expect from you." Liam's posture might have looked relaxed, but she could sense the tension pulsing around him.

"Not everyone is cut out for this life, sweetness. We aren't interested in a 24/7 arrangement, but we're Doms, and that will likely affect all of our interactions."

She was wound too tight to temper the snark in her tone when she asked, "So, what exactly does that mean? What's the difference?"

"Careful, Spitfire, we might decide to keep track of punishments, and you'd be racking them up at a remarkable rate if you'd already said yes." If she'd already said yes, he and Bode would have been providing the relief she'd been seeking from her battery-operated boyfriend.

They'd shown her the second exit, then left her alone to fume over their high-handed behavior. She'd finally fallen asleep just as the sun was coming up. They'd been gone before she made her way into the kitchen. She was edgy from the lack of sleep and from being stuck inside all morning. The note they'd left telling her to take it easy had been the icing on her pissy-attitude cake.

She changed into her running clothes and made her way downstairs midafternoon. Before she could reach the front door, a man she was sure must be seven feet tall stepped in front of her.

"Going somewhere, Colbie?" His deep voice had a rich Texas drawl she'd learned was unique to locals. Whoever he was, he'd been born and raised in the Lone Star state. He loomed over her and she took a step back to save herself a strained neck.

"Yes, I'm going to run off some of my extra energy. It's running or drinking; this seemed like the healthier choice."

He raised a brow at her snarky tone, but she wasn't in the mode to apologize. "Darlin', I'm not the enemy."

"I'll reserve judgement since I don't know you." Okay, so now she was just being a bitch, but her sanity was hanging by a thread and if she had to climb him like a damned tree to get to the door, she would.

"I suppose that's true though I believe you know my wife, Gracie. I'm Jax McDonald." The man's blue eyes sparkled with something close to amusement until his wife's name crossed his lips and then they softened. She'd always been a sucker for a man who loved his wife and immediately felt bad for sniping at him.

"Yes, I've met your wife, she's beautiful... inside and out. I've also heard a lot about her business success. I'm sure you're very proud." He smiled and Colbie was shocked by the transformation. The formidable giant had suddenly turned into an enormous teddy bear.

"Micah and I are both very proud of her. Now that we've made each other's acquaintance, I hope you won't be so averse to taking some advice. Your men aren't going to be pleased with you leaving the building, but I don't see the harm in you running within the compound."

That wasn't going to be a problem because she'd planned to stay close. She had no desire to meet up with the two men who'd been at the garage asking about her. Bored didn't equal suicidal. He shrugged nonchalantly and she saw the corners of his mouth curve up slightly.

"There's a gym at the back of the property with several treadmills. There are several guys in there training, so I doubt the place smells great."

"No thanks." She shuddered. "I deal with sweaty guys all the time at the garage. If I can avoid that, I'd like to. Besides, the fresh air will be good for me." Without responding, he nodded and stepped to the side. She had the strangest feeling she'd just passed some kind of test, but shrugged it off as she made her way down the front staircase.

The whole estate was bathed in bright sunlight, making it look much warmer than it was. Summer was finally over and she was grateful for the break from the stifling heat. At the bottom of the stairs, Colbie began stretching out her muscles, no easy task when her muscles were teaming with tension.

The sound of an approaching vehicle made her stand to see who was approaching. When she recognized the truck, she relaxed and waved at the two men climbing from the one ton dually. Dean and Dell West whistled as they approached her.

"Damn, brother, look what we found. Our favorite mechanic, and it looks like she's getting ready to make a break for it."

"We can't have that. Who'll fix our truck. Gus didn't have a clue what was wrong with it last time. Suppose we should load her up and take her home with us? Once she gets some of that peach cobbler Lilly's making, she'll be happy as a clam at our place." Dell leaned back against the door of their truck and grinned.

Colbie laughed. The two older Wests were born flirts. She suspected it didn't matter if the woman was eight months or eighty, these men would charm them all.

"I was just going for a run. I'm sure escape would be impossible. Mr. McDonald already intercepted me. I've been properly warned off my sinister escape plan."

Dell cupped his hand around his mouth like he was going to share an important conspiracy theory. "There are cameras everywhere, darlin'. Don't even try to escape without our help. And for heaven's sake don't let our lovely wife or sweet daughter-in-law try to help you hatch a plan. God knows those always fail miserably."

"Ain't that the truth? But if you want to stay over at our place and fix up all our wheels, we'll kidnap you. The boys over here may be Uncle Sam's pick for all those top-secret missions, but you never want to forget where they got those smarts." Dean's phone rang and when he pulled it from his pocket, he burst out laughing. "Holy shit. That's a new record." She must have looked as confused as she felt, because he added, "It's a message from Micah informing me kidnapping is a felony."

"Their cameras all have sound, too?" She would have to remember to watch what she said if the place was wired for sight *and* sound.

"Nope. But he and Jax read lips like nobody's business. Jax's deaf sister taught them." Dell shook his head as if it was the most inconvenient thing in the world.

"More like they learned to beat her at the television narration game. They've played that since they were kids. I kind of hated it when Jax started to get better."

"Agreed. His narration was a lot more entertaining when he was making it up on the fly." This time, Dell was chuckling, making Colbie wonder what sort of narration they'd come up with. "Well, we better get inside before the next wave of guards come out. That happens and you'll never get that run." When she looked around trying to decide the best route, Dean called back from the stairs.

"Head around the house and then down the lane to the river. That will be a quarter mile. And from the house to the gate is another quarter mile. That'll make it easy for you to keep track if you're so inclined."

She gave them a wave of thanks and took off.

KENT MET HIS DADS at the top of the stairs. "You two are stone cold. Micah called you, didn't he?"

"Yep. He wanted us to stall Colbie until they could get people in place to watch over her. I don't usually like to play those games, but she's one hell of a mechanic, and we can't be having anything happen to her."

"Besides, it gave us a chance to offer her a better deal. I'm no expert, but that little gal looked about ready to crawl right out of her skin. That tells me she isn't being properly loved and the next best thing is your mama's cobbler." Kent shook his head at Dad Dell's orneriness.

Leave it to him to find the silver lining.

Kent heard a high-pitched squeal from behind him and stepped aside. His wife hadn't seen her fathers-in-law for over a week, and he knew she would be coming in fast. As expected, the petite blonde bombshell he and Kyle called their own, launched herself into the first pair of waiting arms as her tablet clattered to the floor. Thank God they'd finally purchased one of the childproof cases for the high-tech device. She'd gone through several before they finally forced her to secure it in something "Tobi-proof." Picking it up, he interrupted her chattering and asked, "Sweetness, did you walk through the club with this?"

She looked at him over his dad's shoulder and shook her head. "Nope. Gracie did. She said her husbands work all the time, and she hasn't had a good spanking in forever. Something about the two of them needing testosterone supplements. We were looking on-line for them earlier." Kent rolled his eyes. He knew his wife inside and out, she wasn't lying, but she was damned well over-dramatizing the truth. He'd bet his interest in the club she knew Jax was standing behind her.

"God dammit. I swear I don't know which one of you is worse. In this case, the sum is greater than the parts." Jax's growled words made Kent bite the inside of his cheeks to keep from smiling.

"Oh, hi Jax. Guess you've been helping Deaga with her math homework again, huh?"

Kent expected steam to come out of Jax's ears, but the man just shook his head. "It's you. You're the orneriest woman I know—and that's saying a lot considering my wife and Lilly are also vying for the top spot." Shaking his head, he looked up at one of the cameras and growled, "Find her and meet me in the dungeon."

"Kitten, it's a good thing you're standing between our dads, or you might well be headed to the dungeon too." Kyle stepped up and pulled her into his arms and Kent heard him whisper against her ear. "I do believe my brother and I proved last night that we aren't in need of those supplements." Tobi's face flushed a brilliant crimson, and Kent couldn't hold his laughter back any longer.

"You better be nice or I won't share my cobbler with you." Kent stopped laughing and focused his attention on his wife.

"Mom made you a cobbler?"

"Yep." When all four of them stared at her with their mouths gaping open, she shrugged. "She likes me best." *Truer words were never spoken.*

Chapter Seven

COLBIE ROUNDED THE CORNER of the mansion and followed the wide drive toward the back of the property. *Holy cats, this place is a village.* She was shocked at the number of buildings hidden by the enormous building housing the club and penthouse apartment. The forum shops caught her eye, and she made a mental note to check them out during her cool down. Picking up her pace, Colbie focused on following the edge of the winding road.

She passed a gazebo and wondered what sort of kinky uses the Wests had found for the innocent-looking structure. Snorting a laugh to herself, Colbie returned her attention to the road ahead and almost tripped over her own feet when she saw the boat dock. *I wonder if they have jet skis?* She'd always wanted to ride one, but like so many other fun things, her parents had shot the idea down immediately.

Rounding the corner at the end of the dock, Colbie sped up and concentrated on her breathing. She'd been pleasantly surprised to find the fresh air was helping to improve her mood tremendously, but she still needed to burn off some of the residual stress. There were people moving around the compound, but she blocked them out, focusing on the road and the gate by the highway.

A half hour later she was enjoying the rush of endorphins and mopping the sweat from her eyes. She was sprinting every other pass and relishing the burn in her muscles. Exhaustion was starting to take a toll. She considered slowing down, but pushed the idea to the back of her mind. *I need to burn off all that damned lasagna and garlic bread.* Turning, she heard a loud crack as wood splinters from the dock lifted into the air. It took her fatigue soaked brain longer than it should have to register what was happening, and by the time she knew someone was shooting at her, a second shot sent a line of blistering fire along the outside of her shoulder.

Launching herself from the dock, Colbie dove into the water and prayed it was deep enough to keep her from breaking her damned neck. Frigid water engulfed her as she watched a streaking bullet missile through the dim sunlight penetrating the top layers of the river's murky depths. She'd taken a gulping breath of air just before hitting the surface, so she had time to double back under the dock. The structure would offer some protection, and hopefully, whoever was using her as a target wouldn't give her credit for being smart.

Surfacing beneath the dock, Colbie's adrenaline drenched mind scrambled to calculate the trajectory of the bullet she'd seen. If her rusty geometry skills were right, the shooter was on the cliff across the river. She quickly moved behind one of the large pillars, putting the concrete piling between her and the jackass with the gun. Shouting in the distance gave her hope the Prairie Winds Team knew she was ass deep in alligators. Laughing to herself, Colbie wondered what her aristocratic parents would think of how quickly their wayward daughter had adopted Texas' unique vernacular. She loved their colorful expressions, despite her frequent embarrassment when she misinterpreted their meanings. Asking Kent West why he thought she knew anyone who would strangle a toad had quickly become one of her boss's favorite stories.

Trying to stave off hyperventilation, Colbie made a concentrated effort to slow her breathing. Her shoulder was burning, and when she skimmed her hand over the torn flesh, she flinched at the flash of pain. Looking down at her blood covered palm, the world started spinning around her. She'd never been able to cope with the sight of blood, but fainting now meant drowning, so she quickly averted her gaze. Gulping in several deep breaths, Colbie once again concentrated on calming down. Sending up a quick prayer the team found her sooner rather than later, she closed her eyes and leaned her forehead against the rough cement surface of the deck support to await rescue.

LIAM WATCHED MEN run past the windows of conference room, where he was consulting with several team members, seconds before the radio sitting on the long table cackled to life.

Active shooter on the cliff across from the dock. Chopper is in the air and engaged with the sniper and spotter. We've got a female victim in the water people. Find her. There was a pause, and Liam felt the hair on the back of his neck stand on end as Bode grabbed the radio and they all sprinted from the room. He was grateful for the Wests' insistence on drills. The team was prepared for every possible continency—or so he'd thought until Jax's voice came over the radio again. *Liam. Bode. It's Colbie.* With two words, Liam's entire world shifted on its axis.

It took every ounce of discipline he possessed to keep from turning and bolting straight to the dock. Strapping on

Kevlar had never taken so long, and he was about to crawl out of his skin by the time they ran from the armory. One of the compound's souped-up carts sat out front with Kent West behind the wheel. They were moving before Liam's ass hit the seat.

"Security feed shows a shot to her shoulder. The angle is wrong to see if it's a graze or hit. Either way, river water and open wounds don't mix.

"Who's flying the chopper?" Bode had just asked the question floating through Liam's mind.

"Jen. Her men are going apeshit."

Liam could only imagine. There was a reason the rest of the team had dubbed her Miley. The five-foot-nothing blonde was a one-woman wrecking ball. Sam and Sage McCall had their hands full keeping her from taking things down around her. Sam had joked that all she needed to do was walk into a room and pictures fell off the walls. Teaching her to fly had not been one of the Wests' wisest decisions.

"How did that happen?" Liam tried to keep the horror from his voice, but the curve of Kent's lips told him he'd failed.

"She might be a little bit of a thing, but she's damned fast." Kent sounded amused, and Liam wondered if living with Tobi wasn't sapping some of the man's good sense. "She flat outran the rest of the crew and claimed first dibs. Sage made it in time to co-pilot, but Sam is still apoplectic. I swear our insurance rates go up in direct proportion with his blood pressure."

They skidded to a stop behind a short row of trees. Liam owed Kent a huge debt of thanks for giving him something else to focus on while they got into position. Using binoculars, they scanned the area in case the incident was a trap. It was possible the sniper had used Colbie as bait to draw the rest of the team out. Considering the work they did around the world, every member of the team had made powerful enemies.

"Report." Micah's voice came over their earbuds, and they all answered in turn. Quartering the compound allowed them to study a smaller area and give the all-clear sooner. "Get in there and find her. Start under the dock."

Liam agreed. It was the most logic choice, considering how open the area was. Except for the short expanse of trees where they'd parked, the riverbank along the back of the compound was routinely cleared, to discourage intruders, but in this instance, any additional cover would have been a blessing.

Before they could jog the last hundred yards, Jen's excited voice burst out of his earbud, making Liam stumble. "Holy shit balls, babe, did you see that? Hang on."

"He's going to paddle her ass." Kent's amused chuckle came from beside him, and Liam shook his head. "I swear she'd intentionally throw rocks at a bear. She and Tobi are cut from the same cloth. We were already considering having genetic testing done to make sure they aren't long-lost sisters, and now, we need to add Colbie to the mix. Maybe Joelle Morgan will give us a group discount."

Liam shook his head at Kent's chattering and wondered if they had really talked the Nobel Prize winner into testing the women. They looked up just as a man jumped from the cliff into the river. The small, but agile Prairie Winds helicopter appeared over the cliff seconds later. It went into a dive Liam bet lifted both pilots out of their seats. Sage McCall's colorful cursing confirmed he wasn't happy with his wife's daredevil flying.

The roar of a boat motor resounded off the rock wall,

and Liam worried the sniper had just made his escape. "My bird is faster than your boat, asshat." He wasn't sure what was louder, the roar of the boat's motor, the chopper, or Sam's vehement orders for Jen to stand down.

"Never a dull moment. Now, let's go get your girl." Liam couldn't have agreed more.

BODE WAS ABOUT to go out of his mind with worry, and suddenly, the entire team seemed to have turned into a bunch of comedians. Kicking off his boots at the edge of the dock, he dropped over the edge, feet first. Surfacing seconds later, he opened his eyes just in time to see Colbie duck under the water. He reached beneath the surface and pulled her up by the front of her shirt. Her eyes were wild, and she fought against his hold until he gave her a quick shake. "It's me, Storeen. Stop."

The moment his words penetrated her fear, she went limp. He pulled her into his arms and let relief wash over him. As soon as his arms closed around her, Colbie began shaking so violently, he knew she was going into shock. Pushing off the coarse surface of the pillar, he moved them both toward the shore where Liam and Kent were already wading toward them. Liam held a blanket open in his arms, and Bode shifted her into his hold.

Ten minutes later, they were in the back of an ambulance, speeding toward the local hospital, despite Colbie's fervent objections. She still hadn't spoken, but her agitation had increased the bleeding from the deep graze.

"Spitfire, we won't leave your side. The only doctors we'll allow to treat you are members of the club. They've already been briefed and have assured us they've secured the area."

She was shaking so hard, Bode worried she was going to do more damage to her arm and was about to ask the paramedics to restrain her when he felt the vehicle slowing down. Colbie was close to hysterical by the time they wheeled her through the sliding doors of the emergency entrance. Dr. Kirk Evans met them in the reception area and led them back to an examination room close to a secondary exit.

Leaning over the gurney, Kirk cupped her wet cheeks with his large hands, forcing her to look only at him. "Colbie, I'm Kirk Evans. You and I met a couple of months ago when you fixed my wife's car." Bode was relieved to see her nod in understanding. "My partner, Brian Bennett, will be here in a few minutes. The two of us are the only ones who'll be in this room aside from the Prairie Winds Team, do you understand?"

To Bode's enormous relief, she whispered, "Yes, Sir." and the violent shaking began to abate.

"I'm going to unwrap the blanket. I want to look at your arm and make sure we don't need anything I haven't already prepared for." Those words made Bode look around him, and for the first time, he noted the numerous trays of supplies lining a nearby counter. Taking a step back, he eased open a door to find a large bathroom, complete with a shower he wished like hell he could get in—damn it, he hated the smell of river water.

As if the Universe had been listening, Kirk looked up and smiled. "Help yourself. She'll join you in just a minute. I need you both cleaned up before the Director of Nursing comes down here to kick our asses. No offense, but you smell like a river rat, and you're dripping all over the floor. I'll cover her wound and let her take a quick shower while we wait for Brian."

Liam grinned looking down at his own wet jeans and boots. "I'll round us up some clothes. I'm an easier fix, so you go in with her. Kirk is right about the stench." Bode agreed. The part of the river where the water had been moving hadn't been rank, but close to the bank, the smell of dying foliage as summer faded to fall had been overwhelming.

Walking back to Colbie's bedside, he pulled her hand to his lips and smiled down at her. "I'll get the shower warmed up for you, sweetness. We'll get you cleaned up, so the doc can stitch you up, and we can get home. I swear I aged a decade before we could get to you." Those few minutes waiting for the order to go had been the longest of his life.

Five minutes later, Liam led her into the bathroom and gave her a quick kiss before handing her off to Bode. "I'll back in a few minutes with towels and clothes. Kent's already rounded up most of it." He gave Bode a knowing look when he noticed he was still wearing his boxers.

Colbie took a tentative step into the large enclosure and groaned when the warm water washed over her bare legs. Liam handed him a pair of scissors and then disappeared out the door. Cutting away her clothing gave him more pleasure than it should have, given the circumstances. He'd already vowed to buy her a new wardrobe, so he didn't feel any guilt about tossing the shredded clothing into the trash. As each square inch of her creamy skin was exposed, Bode was more grateful he'd left his boxers on. The thin cotton might not be a huge barrier, but it was enough to remind him she deserved better than a quick fuck in a hospital shower.

"You steal my breath, my sweet Storeen." Kneeling in

front of her to pull the last of her clothing free, Bode pressed kisses along the ridge of her pelvic bone. Her neatly trimmed blonde curls sparkled as water droplets clung to them. *Pretty, but they have to go.*

Nuzzling her mound, he spoke against her wet skin, "Even soaked in river water, you smell like a tasty treat, and I can't wait to feast on you. Since I plan to spend hours enjoying our first time together, we're going to finish this shower as quickly as possible—because you are a temptation I'm barely able to refuse."

Standing, he helped her turn her back to the water and angled her so the water wasn't falling on her left shoulder. "Lean your head back, and I'll wash your hair." She groaned when his fingers massaged her scalp. Chuckling at her response, he leaned forward and kissed the shell of her ear. "I promise to give you a massage that will make you sleep like a baby, sweetness."

"And if I don't want to sleep?" She reached back to smooth her right hand along his thigh and the rush of blood to his cock almost made him lightheaded.

"Fuck." His groan was a plea for mercy rather a request. "You're playing with fire, baby, and we can't do this here." Her hand dropped so quickly, he knew he'd hurt her feelings. He felt like an ass when she refused to look him in the eye, and he saw the red stain of embarrassment coloring her cheeks. By the time he'd finished his own shower, she'd stepped out and wrapped herself in a towel—a move he was sure had caused her a lot of pain. Blood stained the wrap Kirk had secured over the gash, and she looked pale.

When Liam stepped into the room, he must have felt the tension because the look he gave Bode was full of accusation. "Come, Spitfire. I'll help you dress."

Bode cupped the back of her neck and pulled her close. "Not the time and not the place, but don't ever question how much I want you, Colbie." He'd deliberately used her name rather than a term of endearment. She needed to know how serious he was about his desire for her. The relief a quick shagging would have provided would have faded quickly. They'd both have regretted it later, and he wanted to begin on the right foot.

He dressed quickly and shook his head at Kent West's resourcefulness. How the man had gotten him clothing and boots in the span of ten minutes was a testament to how connected Kent and Kyle West were. By the time he stepped into the exam room, Colbie was laying back on the raised exam table. She was dressed in yoga pants and a halter top. She was trembling, so he pulled a blanket from the warmer and spread it over her legs. She murmured her thanks as he leaned forward to press a kiss against her forehead.

Brian Bennett was examining her wound, a frown wrinkling his brow. "I want to do this in layers, Colbie. It'll help reduce the scarring, but it'll be a bitch if we don't get ahead of the infection, so we're going to frontload you with antibiotics." When she didn't respond, he paused and looked at her. "I'm a Dom, sweetie, so I'll expect you to respond even if I don't ask you a direct question. I want to know you understand what I'm saying. Medical treatment is like play in that it's about compliance and communication. I can't do my job unless I know it's what you want. Ultimately, it's all in your hands."

"Yes. I mean, yes, I understand, Sir. As long as you don't give me penicillin, I'll be fine."

Brian nodded and turned to the laptop sitting on the counter. "I'm starting a record for you, but this computer isn't connected to the hospital's system. Merilee will cover our tracks with the hospital."

Kent's smile drew Colbie's attention and he nodded toward Brian. "What Dr. Bennett didn't mention is that Merilee Lanham, one of the hospital's administrators, is a member of the club. We look out for each other. Even when it means bending the rules a bit." Understanding dawned in her eyes, and she nodded.

"Thank you," she said, turning back to Brian. "I appreciate all you're doing to keep me safe. Hospitals are dangerous places for someone like me."

She was right. Medical facilities, by necessity, gathered personal information and were notorious for breaches of security. Bode knew the team used Kirk and Brian's clinic whenever possible because their medical records system had been designed by Micah Drake and Phoenix Morgan. Phoenix was one of the most sought-after programmers in the world, and Bode was sure there wasn't a system around Micah hadn't broken in to. *And there's no one better to help design a secure system than a hacker.*

Chapter Eight

COLBIE GLARED AT the thermostat on the opposite wall, trying to block out the pinches as they deadened the scratch on her arm. Personally, she thought they were making a really big deal about something she would have taped shut with a few sports Band-Aids. When she'd said as much, she'd gotten dark glowers from all five Doms in the room. One thing she'd learned hanging out at the track in London and working for Gus… some days it just didn't pay to argue with men.

Dr. Kirk had given her two injections. The first he'd explained was the loading dose of antibiotics they'd discussed. When she inquired about the second shot, he'd grinned. She'd been shocked by the startling change the smile made. His whole demeanor shifted from formidable to approachable.

"This is going to make you like me a lot more than you do now." He must have noticed her surprise, because he'd added, "It's okay, sweet girl. I'm used to being seen as scary. My wife tells me I don't smile enough."

"And he tells her she isn't naked enough." All the men laughed at Dr. Brian's comment. Colbie envied what was obviously a close friendship. Even before her life had been turned upside down, she hadn't had any close friends. The women in her social class were snobs and concerned with little, aside from shopping and marrying well. The women who spent time at the track were jealous of her rapport with the men and treated her as an interloper. Shaking off the loneliness threatening to float over her like a dark cloud, she realized she'd actually shaken her head so hard, she was suddenly dizzy.

"Careful, sweet girl. The sedative I gave you could affect your balance. We don't want you falling off the table—too much paperwork." Dr. Kirk's face was in front of her, and she silently agreed with his wife… he should smile more.

Letting her mind drift back over the events of the day, Colbie tuned out conversation around her. It wasn't until she heard an agitated female voice outside the door, she realized she'd closed her eyes.

"I love you to pieces, Tank, but if you don't move, I'm going to take you apart."

Colbie recognized Tobi West's voice and chuckled at her empty threat. She'd met Tank, and his nickname was well earned. As a former NFL star, he was huge. Thinking about the petite blonde "taking him apart" made Colbie snicker again.

Kirk Evans looked at Kent and grinned. "You should probably rescue him. I'd hate to see her hurt him. We're already busy with one club member, no need to double our workload."

Kent opened the door and pulled Tobi into his arms. "Sweetness, are you threatening the employees again? You know Tank is terrified of you. Hell, he'll probably have nightmares for a week. Do you really want that on your conscience?"

Colbie watched in disbelief until the irony was too much and she burst out laughing. "Holy hell, this is better than any sitcom I've ever seen." When she turned quickly to Liam, she almost fell off the table, and Kirk Evans made a noise that sounded a lot like a growl. Turning back to him, she leaned precariously close to his face and asked. "Did you just snarl at me? Because it sounded like it, and I'm pretty sure that's a no-no in most etiquette books. I'd have to double-check, but I'm almost sure I read that snarling was forbidden." His face swam in front of her, but even with him moving, she could see the corners of his mouth twitching.

"I want you to hold still, sweetness. I'm not sure your men want Kirk and I to be the first ones to bind you." His gaze shifted somewhere over her head, but when she tried to turn strong hands held her still. She felt another pinch in her arm and things began to fade quickly. The last thing she heard was Tobi's voice.

"Don't look at me that way, Master. I'm not letting him near me with a needle."

LIAM WATCHED THE LIGHT fade from Colbie's eyes as he eased her back against the pillow. Judging by her blank stare, she hadn't realized he was the one holding her. In an eye-opening moment of self-awareness, it occurred to him how much that mattered. He'd wanted her to know she was being sheltered in his arms—that Bode had been right beside him, holding her hips, so she hadn't rolled off the damned table.

"Holy craptastic, I thought she was going to take a header off that platform. No offense guys, but that thing looks way too much like a morgue table. All that stainless steel... yikes." Tobi shuddered, and Liam had to smile. She'd just said exactly what he'd been thinking since they first walked into the room.

"In hindsight, we should have put her in one of the other rooms. They have rails on the beds. But like my dad always said, hindsight is twenty-twenty." Brian had already returned to work, placing the under layer of stitches.

"We wanted her as far from the front entrance as possible to give your guys plenty of time to deal with anyone walking through the door set on finding her. With the secondary exit nearby, this was perfect."

"Did the lights here dim? I swear when Micah fires up all those fucking gadgets, the local electric company goes apeshit, and they have to throw some auxiliary power switch. Like that Christmas movie where the alarm sounds and warning lights go off when Clark put all those damned lights on his house? Micah pulled a good shot of that asshole sniper's face off the dock feed. He and Phoenix are running facial recognition programs at some Mach speed Jax said would have the console smokin' in no time. If somebody has to call the fire department, make sure they know it's not me this time."

Tobi was talking a mile a minute, completely unaware of her husband rolling his eyes toward heaven at her profanity-laced chatter. With her back to the door, she hadn't noticed her other husband step into the room either.

"Kitten." With just one word, Kyle West silenced his wife and made every man in the room chuckle at her whispered curse. Liam was almost certain her comment about a duck wasn't anatomically possible. Kyle had once told him, no matter what they tried, they hadn't been able to break her habit of cursing when she was excited.

Tobi looked around the room, leveling each of them with a look that would likely make most men cover their family jewels. She wasn't pleased with the amused looks on the faces surrounding her.

"You all knew he was there and didn't tell me? Boy, oh boy. Rats... you're all rats. I swear, I'm getting voodoo dolls made to look like every Dom at the club and then sponsoring the biggest margarita party ever for the subs. I'll surf eBay until I find enough hat pins to torture you all and then it'll be on. You just wait and see." Every man in the room flinched, and Kyle rolled his eyes behind her.

"You are incorrigible, kitten. Let Brian work, the team is getting antsy to get Colbie back to the compound. Even though having her on our home turf didn't help us much earlier today."

"I told you buying the land across the river wasn't going to help unless we fenced it off." Kent's comment about purchasing the adjacent tract was obviously news to everyone in the room—including their wife.

"The dads were reviewing the bids, but I assure you, they've kicked it into high gear now." Kyle moved his gaze between Liam and Bode as he added, "I'm sorry. There isn't anything else I can say. She did exactly what Jax asked her to do. She turned around well before the gate near the road and several feet shy of the end of the dock. She'd have expected an attack to come from the road, not the river."

The path she'd run would have kept her sheltered from view for all but a few seconds as she turned on the dock. Whoever the shooter was, he was either damned lucky, or he was familiar with the layout of the compound. The last thought was damned humbling.

Kyle shifted his weight in a move Liam suspected was to relieve some of the frustration he was feeling. When he held out his hand, Tobi walked into his arms and hugged him tightly.

"This is all on that jerk who shot at Colbie. Don't you

be feeling like you didn't do enough, I just won't have it." Kyle's expression softened as he leaned down to press a kiss against the top of her pale blonde hair.

"Every man in the world should have a woman who loves as unconditionally as you do, kitten. I'm convinced it would be a much nicer place if we all experienced such selfless support."

Liam felt a pang of jealousy and sent up a silent prayer he and Bode would someday have a relationship like the Wests.

"But that doesn't mean I've forgotten all your cursing, kitten." Pulling back, Kyle frowned down at Tobi. "We'll deal with that later."

"I have it on good authority the kids are going to the movies with mom this evening." Kent's smirk made Liam choke back a laugh.

"Traitor." Tobi's glare earned her a scathing look from Kent. Liam knew the man might look like a soft touch, but his core was pure sexual dominant—something he suspected Tobi forgot regularly. "Sorry, Sir."

"Jesus, Joseph, and Mary, people. Can you take this outside? I'm never going to finish this with the Lucy Show playing in here."

Kirk snorted a laugh at Brian's comment before opening the door and urging the Wests into the hall. The last thing Liam heard was Tobi giggling.

"I can't believe we got kicked out for talking. That hasn't happened to me in…. well, at least a couple of weeks."

Shaking his head, Brian returned to his work. "I swear she and the other women at the Prairie Winds Club are the most resilient people I know. They've all been through so much, but they burst through the other side, smiles in place and ready to take on the world. It's remarkable."

"I've seen the close friendship between them; what role does that play in their recovery?" Liam was surprised by Bode's question. Not that he hadn't considered that angle, but his friend wasn't usually as interested in the finer points of social interaction. Bode had definitely been born on the wrong side of the pond and a century too late. He was more the shoot now and ask questions later type—it was probably part of the reason he'd fit in with the team of former Special Forces soldiers so quickly.

"I'm sure that's a large part of it." Brian didn't look up from the row of sutures he was finishing up when Kirk stepped back into the room. "They have a built-in support system. As I see it, they are a very special group. They've all experienced unique traumas and are submissives who have a built-in need to please others. Someone who doesn't understand the full range of nuances of the lifestyle might see the stiff upper lip routine as strength. Whereas, another sub understands and offers a safe place to vent. Without friends who understand, a submissive would probably bottle up all that emotion because they wouldn't want to trouble anyone."

"Granted, I'm walking into the middle of this conversation, but I can't begin to tell you how important Tobi and Gracie's friendship has been to Regi. Even though she worked at the club, she hadn't fully embraced the lifestyle because she was afraid to let go and trust. Those two women had her back when everything was collapsing around her. They hold a special place in our hearts for all their support." Kirk chuckled before adding, "And they're damned entertaining, too. Personally, I hope Tobi does get a margarita party together. We all watch from the control room; those women are a hoot."

"You're just saying that because they always end up naked." When Liam turned abruptly back to Brian, he shrugged. "It's true. They usually end up skinny dipping."

"And you encourage this?" Liam couldn't hold the note of judgement from his voice.

"Hell, yes." They answered in unison with nearly identical disbelieving looks. "What's not to love? Beautiful, naked women having the time of their lives, racking up punishments like it was a competition. It doesn't get any better." Kirk's laughter was loud enough to elicit a reaction from Colbie. When she tried to roll away from Kirk's voice, he patted her hand and apologized. "Sorry, sweetie."

Kirk handed Liam a sheet of instructions, including the prescriptions he'd already called in to a local pharmacy. "One of us will come back to town for these after we've gotten Colbie settled."

"No need," the doctor shook his head. "Merilee came by, she and Tobi are taking care of it. Kyle sent Tank with them—I'm not sure if it was for their protection or to keep the two of them out of trouble."

"I don't know what they pay him," Bode shrugged, "but there's no way in hell it's enough."

"I asked Kent about that once, and he assured me the women were making Tank a very rich man. He gets bonuses every time he keeps Tobi out of jail." Brian looked up as he affixed the last strip of tape to the dressing and smiled. "I referred him to our financial manager, figuring he had a lot of extra cash drawing zip-squat interest in a savings account. It turns out, Tank is a closet stock trader. I'm thinking of turning my portfolio over to him."

Chapter Nine

Bode sat slumped in the chair at the side of the bed, watching Colbie sleep. He'd carried her out of the hospital and held her until Liam had taken her from his arms once they'd been safely inside the garage. She'd opened her eyes when they first stepped from the elevator; the brief flash of alarm at the realization she was being carried by a man, faded quickly as she took in her surroundings. He'd wanted to fist pump knowing she'd felt comfortable enough to fall back asleep in Liam's arms.

He'd sworn he was going to keep his enthusiasm in check, but everything about Colbie called to him. On the surface, she appeared tough and acutely aware of the danger she was facing. But underneath, there was a core of vulnerability he couldn't resist. The first time he'd seen her, he'd known she was scared out of her mind, but her determination to push past it showed a soul who was wise far beyond her years.

Over the past year, he and Liam had meticulously reviewed every aspect of her background. She might have blood the color of Texas Bluebells, but their families routinely made the Forbes's list, despite their fathers' best efforts to throw the publication off their trails. Bode's parents swore the magazine's list painted a target on them which every thief in the world could see. Liam's family was even more cautious, but so far, their efforts to conceal their wealth from the media had proven futile.

Over the years, they'd been targeted by two types of women. Those who wanted to know what if felt like to have two men focused on their sexual pleasure. They'd sworn they could handle the commitment involved, that they could handle the dominant sides of his and Liam's personalities, but those promises had always quickly fallen apart. Most hadn't made it out of the bedroom before the reality of dealing with two sexual Dominants settled over them like a dark cloud.

Other women were only concerned with their bank balance. It didn't matter how normally they tried to live, the media took great pleasure in publishing the details of their trust funds' annual growth. The truth was, most of those writers knew more about his money than he did. *God knows they're more interested.*

Shifting in his seat, Bode scrubbed his hand over his face, hoping to push aside the fatigue threatening to pull him under. Dropping his hand, his gaze went back to the woman in front of him. He was surprised to see her watching him, her crystalline blue eyes drowsy with sleep, but the fog of drugs had cleared. For several seconds, he simply enjoyed the moment. He was sure she underestimated how beautiful she was. Sky-high cheekbones and a perfectly shaped nose covered in pristine ivory skin so soft he longed to kiss every inch, Guinevere Colbert-Lister was, in a word, stunning. Her long blonde waves had been an invitation few men would have been able to resist, but those had been replaced with short red spikes which did little to conceal the startling beauty they topped.

"Are you okay?" Her quiet question pulled him from his musings, and he smiled.

"I think I'm the one who should be asking that question although I know you aren't really okay—at least not yet." Her gentle smile made his breath catch. Pushing from the chair, he stretched and then stepped up to the bed. Sitting beside her, Bode smoothed his hand over her cheek. "Give me a number for the pain, Storeen." Her quick glance to the side told him she planned to underplay her discomfort. "Don't lie to me, sweetheart, because I assure you that I'll know."

She took a deep breath before answering, "My arm is throbbing, but I don't want to take anything that will knock me out. I already feel like I have the world's worst hangover, and I only want to fight this once." When her eyes became watery with tears, he wanted to growl with frustration.

"Let's try a half dose of the pain killer Kirk prescribed. I'll make you some toast first, so it doesn't upset your stomach." When she tried to sit up, tears poured down her cheeks. "Hold on. Let me help." He slipped his arms under her knees and behind her back to set her gently on the edge of the bed. Without asking, he helped her into the bathroom.

When he didn't leave the room, she blinked up at his in confusion. "Aren't you going to leave?"

"No."

"What? Really? What about privacy? I can't pee with you standing there." He held back his grin when she stood stock still like a deer caught in the headlights. "Call it performance anxiety, but I won't be able to do it. Can you please just stand on the other side of the door?"

He wanted to push the issue, but she was already swaying on her feet. Bode believed in the old adage about beginning as you intend to go, but he also knew there was wisdom in choosing your battles.

"I'll be right outside the door. Don't stand up until I'm beside you." Since he knew she wasn't wearing anything beneath the sundress they'd slipped her into hours ago, she didn't need to be embarrassed by him helping with panties. Smiling to himself as he stepped outside the door, he enjoyed knowing she'd have little need for panties once she was theirs. Well, aside from the fact he loved the sound of lace being ripped apart.

She called his name a few seconds later, and his heart stuttered at the sweet sound. Back at Colbie's side, Bode steadied her as she stood up and swayed precariously on her feet. After she'd finished freshening up, he led her slowly into the living room. Liam had heard them coming down the hall and already had pillows and blankets waiting on the sofa. Stress lines from the pain bracketed her mouth by the time she was settled.

"I'll make the toast while Liam pampers you." He'd often teased his friend about being a mother hen; it would do them both good to spend time together. By the time he returned, she was already fading. "Oh no you don't. You need something to eat before you get a nap. If Tobi shows up and finds out we haven't fed you, she'll make extra voodoo dolls of us."

Colbie wrinkled her brow trying to figure out what he meant and Liam laughed.

"She threatened to make the dolls because no one told her Kyle was standing behind her at the hospital. I'm certain her profanity-laced tirade earned her more than a few swats."

"Tobi mentioned that her men are sticklers about that, but I didn't know why."

"To outsiders, I'm sure it looks like they are trying to control her language and dictate what she can and cannot say, but that's not it. They simply want her to be the best she can be and talking like a drunken sailor isn't going to earn her the respect they both feel she deserves."

Liam's explanation was spot-on as far as Bode was concerned. Most Doms had rules against their subs cursing, and their reasons varied, but he knew Kent and Kyle were entirely focused on what was best for Tobi. After finishing her toast, he handed her the medication, but she held it in her hand without taking it.

"Yes. I mean, the answer you wouldn't let me give you last night… or" she was looking around for a clock, and Bode realized she had no idea how much time had passed since she'd been shot.

"Our conversation was two nights ago, sweetheart."

"Holy shi…ne. I slept that long? What the heck did they give me?"

"Good save on the language," Bode smiled. "We'll ask that you curb the cursing as much as possible, but we also know those changes take time. As for what they gave you, you'll need to check with Kirk, but I know it hit you much harder than he expected. I'm sure he's made notations in your chart, but it's information you need to have as well."

"Whatever." Liam waved his hand in a motion of impatience. "Let's get back to the part where she said yes before she takes that pill."

"I'd already said yes, but you wouldn't accept my answer. I'm just repeating what I said earlier. I've been given another second chance, and I don't want to waste it."

He had a deep sense of what she wasn't saying as well. She didn't think she was going to be able to stay in Texas, and she wanted to enjoy what time she had with them.

"I'd like to learn more about the lifestyle, but it's been a long time since I had the training class, so you'll have to be patient."

Bode wanted to laugh and rail at the same time about her request for patience. It seemed like they'd been waiting forever, so a few more days wouldn't hurt.

"We'll go as slow as you need for us to go. But I want you to notice I said we'd be addressing your *needs* and those may not always line up with what you think you want."

Bode agreed with what Liam said and nodded to show her he was on the same page. He crossed his arms over his chest, drawing her attention.

"I'd like to add I don't think there is any class that would adequately prepare you for having two Doms." Her eyes were wide, but he didn't see any sign of fear or uncertainty in them.

She took a deep breath and then nodded. "Maybe Tobi could help me. She has two men." Bode felt his jaw drop and for the first time in years, he was struck dumb.

"I'm not sure I've ever seen Bode speechless." Liam leaned his head back and laughed.

"What's wrong with asking Tobi?" The little minx's grin told him she was being intentionally naïve.

"Not a thing, sweetheart. By all means, ask Tobi your questions. Follow her lead. I'll enjoy having your bare ass draped over my lap. Hell, my palm is itching in anticipation of seeing it's imprint turn a lovely shade of pink against your creamy skin." Bode watched her pupils dilate and heard the small catch in her breathing. The dress she wore exposed the base of her throat, and he watched her pulse kick up. She shuddered under his scrutiny, and he caught the flinch of pain she tried valiantly to hide.

"Take your medication, Spitfire. Fighting the pain will only slow the healing process. Now that you've agreed to be ours, we're going to make sure you take better care of yourself." Liam was right, she'd done very little to make her small apartment feel like home. And what they'd found in her kitchen barely qualified as food.

"Can I take a nap out here?" She hesitated, and he could see she was debating whether or not to continue. "I... well, I don't want to be by myself." She nodded to the table where Liam had been working. "I know you both have work to do and..." Her words trailed off, and Bode stepped forward to tip her chin up until her eyes focused on his.

"First lesson. You will never be punished or thought less of for telling us what you need. Eventually, we'll be able to anticipate most of those needs, but we'll never get it right one hundred percent of the time."

Liam had moved in so that his chest was pressed against Colbie's back. Bode watched as he leaned down to speak close to her ear.

"This will only work if you're honest with yourself and with us. You'll find we are quite accommodating if you are respectful with your requests. Quite accommodating, indeed." Her throaty moan made both men smile as they settled her on the large living room sofa.

Bode watched her eyelids close as if they were in slow motion and within seconds, the rhythmic sound of her breathing told him she was already fast asleep. Feeling his friend's scrutiny, he looked up at Liam and shrugged.

"I'm trying to hold back, I know I should, but there is something about her that's a magnet to my steel. Hell, I've spent the better part of the past twenty-four hours just watching her sleep and the pull has gotten stronger." *If I'm falling this fast when she's sleeping, I'm fucking doomed when we finally get her between us.*

Chapter Ten

TOBI KNOCKED ON her husbands' office door and waited. It had always seemed odd to knock when they lived in the building, but now that they'd moved into their own home, it wasn't nearly as difficult to remember. *And remembering reaps rewards.* Kyle shouted for her to enter and she took a deep breath and pulled open the heavy wooden door. Stepping inside the oversized space, she was surprised to see he was alone. He didn't look up until he heard the lock on the door snick; the sound seemed louder than usual in the silence.

A dark smile filled with promise spread over his handsome face, and Tobi felt her breath catch. She would have thought the intensity of her attraction to her men would fade over time, but the opposite seemed to be true. Moments like this, she could only stand and stare at the handsome man looking at her like he wanted to lay her out on his desk and devour her. As mirror image twins, both her men looked like they should be gracing magazine covers rather than running a kink club. She still wondered about those who couldn't seem to tell them apart. That had never been an issue for her. She'd never confused them, even when they'd tried to fool her.

Shaking off her mind's wandering, Tobi was surprised to find he was no longer sitting behind the mammoth hunk of oak he called a desk. Leaning against a dark leather sofa facing the fireplace, he stood watching her. She felt her cheeks heat when she realized she was staring at him like he was an afternoon snack. But dammit to doorknobs, he was delicious and all she could think about was how much she wanted to taste him. Every. Single. Inch.

Her body had been hijacked by the hormones surging through her veins and every nerve ending fired in unison, making her skin tingle. When her nipples peaked, the lacy bra and silk blouse she wore did little to hide them from his view. She saw his pupils dilate when his gaze fell to her chest. She'd given up trying to figure out what men as good looking as Kyle and Kent could possibly see in her. Now she just counted it as a blessing and thanked her lucky stars every day that she'd barged into a meeting between her boss and Lilly West.

The local magazine Tobi had worked for was interested in the club the West's were opening, but Kent West had dodged her requests for an interview for weeks. Her chance encounter with his mother was the reason Tobi was standing here today. She'd been on her way to the interview Lilly made possible when the torrential rain from a sudden thunderstorm sent her small car hydroplaning into a water-filled ditch. Attempts to flag down passing cars from the side of the road had proven futile, so she'd stood defiantly in the middle of the highway. Kyle had nearly run over her and the fireworks that followed had been the tip of the iceberg. The chemistry between the three of them was undeniable and incendiary.

"I don't know what you're thinking, kitten, but your breathing just kicked up, and I can see the flush of arousal spreading over your exposed chest. I do love your low-cut blouses. Not only because they give me sweet peeks at the lusciousness awaiting me, they also let me see that first evidence of desire moving over your flawless skin. The rapid rise and fall of your breasts as your breathing shallows pushes the peaks of your nipples temptingly into the silk. But it's your eyes that tell me you've gone to a memory that's sent sweet cream to your pussy. I know if I reached under that scrap of material you call a skirt, I'd be able to slide my fingers between your wet folds and pull them back coated with the evidence of your need."

Everything he'd said was true. Every word. He hadn't even touched her, and she was already skating dangerously on the edge of orgasm. The man was her Master in every sense of the word, but he often reminded her that his real power lay in his love for her. She knew it was true… he gave her exactly what she needed. Her biggest hurdle as a submissive was accepting their definitions of *need* weren't always the same.

Forcing herself back to the moment, she took a deep breath and squared her shoulders. The corners of Kyle's lips twitched, and if she didn't know him as well as she did, she would have missed it. The small *tell* let her know he recognized her switching mental gears. When she didn't move, he held out his hand to her. He hadn't needed to speak. The small gesture had been enough to call her to his side. Standing in front of him, she relaxed. The tension she'd felt under his scrutiny always fell away when he touched her. His chocolate eyes were warm with a love she hadn't believed was possible before she met the two of them.

"That brilliant mind of yours is wandering again, kitten. Let's see if we can't get you to focus, shall we?" He widened his stance and pulled her between his legs until she was flush against his chest. Wrapping her long hair around his fist until it tugged at her scalp, Kyle made certain her focus was centered on him. His tight hold on her hair sent tingles of pain dancing over the roots and forced her attention to zero in on the man lowering his lips to her. Just before they connected, he smiled down at her.

"There's the look every Dom loves, all your thoughts directed on your Master. Anticipation sending those delicious endorphins coursing through your blood. Your body was already responding to me, and now that your mind isn't spinning out of control, it's catching up as well."

He was right, her body was balanced on the precipice, and his words were a large splash of gasoline onto the fire. Kyle had proven time and again he could make her come with words alone. Add in the small bite of pain and the underlying feeling of being bound? Yep, she was toast. His lips brushed back and forth over hers with a featherlight touch, making her want to tangle her fingers in his hair and pull him close, so she could plunder his mouth and claim him all over again.

The citrus mint smell of his favored mints filled her senses, the scent unique to him and one she associated with intimacy. She'd once read that a person's sense of smell was a huge memory trigger and her Masters made it easy to believe.

"There you go again, my love. Time to step up my game if your mind has time for a field trip." Sealing his lips over hers, he stole her breath and every thought. Nothing existed outside of his kiss. Probing every corner of her mouth, his tongue was relentless in its exploration. Tobi found herself just hanging on for the ride.

KYLE FOUGHT HIS SMILE as Tobi pressed herself against the

hard ridge of his erection. Damn, she was so wonderfully wanton; he often wondered what he and his brother had done to deserve her. She had a mind as sharp as anyone he'd ever met, and her loyalty to those she loved was unfailing. He'd never known Tobi to dislike anyone without a solid reason. Their parents adored her and their children thought their mama hung the moon—he and Kent agreed. She was a natural submissive who challenged them daily because she craved the reassurance they cared enough to rein her in.

After her mother died when she was seven years old, the only attention Tobi had gotten was cruel beatings her father had administered. Her older brother escaped to college, and his indifference had crushed her. Kyle still beat the shit out of the bag in the gym anytime he thought about her father chaining her to the walls and thrashing her with anything he could lay his hands on. The only thing that kept him and Kent from killing the bastard was that he was already dead.

He could feel the heat of Tobi's sex through his jeans and the heady scent of her arousal surrounded him. He couldn't count the number of times since she'd entered their lives he'd nearly come in his pants. Damn, the woman made him feel like an out-of-control teenager most of the time.

One of the things he loved about sharing her with his brother was knowing they could play off one another when their control was too close to the edge. Their twin bond was strong enough that verbal communication wasn't usually required. Hell, Kent was probably cursing like the sailor now because he'd was stuck in Houston waiting for the weather to clear enough so he could fly home. They'd taken off a few minutes ago, and Kent was faunching at the bit to get back to Tobi. How his mother had talked him into flying her to the Gulf was a mystery to Kyle. All he knew was she was working on something special for their dads for their upcoming sixtieth birthdays, and she'd wanted to approve the final plans personally. Why it was urgent when the party was still ten months away, he didn't know.

"Now who's the one whose mind is wandering?"

Christ, when had she stopped kissing him? Growling a wicked promise against the shell of her ear, he turned her quickly and bent her over the desk. Lifting her skirt, he smiled when he saw the thong she wasn't supposed to be wearing.

"Oh, kitten. What were you thinking coming to me with panties on?" Her only response was a gasp when he ripped what was probably an expensive piece of lace from her quivering body. He didn't give her a chance to spread herself for him, he simply kicked her feet apart. "Arch your back bad girl. Covering your pussy means those swollen folds are going to feel the sting of the swats you've earned."

She thrust back until her sex was completely exposed to the fall of his palm. The first strike sent her up onto her toes, and she moaned. Damn, she was so fucking perfect, he wasn't sure he'd ever stop thanking God he'd sent her to them. He pulled his throbbing cock out from behind the zipper of his jeans between swats, partly to be sure he was ready to fuck her, but he also wanted to avoid the permanent damage the damned metal teeth were doing to a body part he had big plans for.

After the third swat, he bent down and bit the hot flesh. She'd have a mark, but he'd been careful to avoid breaking the skin. She screamed his name in the way she knew made him completely insane. Moving behind her, he pushed between the swollen folds and smiled as he watched his cock disappear between the glistening, scarlet tissues. When he pressed against her cervix, she groaned and rippled around him.

"Christ. You are so fucking hot. I don't have the words to tell you how incredible it feels, kitten. All of those lovely muscles pulsing around me as your heat sucks all logical thought from my mind."

"Please, oh please, fuck me, Master. I need to know how much you want me."

The last bit made him snarl. "Want you? Kitten, I can scarcely breathe without you." And it was true. Tobi owned him, heart and soul. He still hadn't found out why she'd come to his office, but that was going to have to wait. Right now, his wife deserved his undivided attention. Whatever had led up to that whispered admission was about to be pushed so far out of her mind she wouldn't remember a time when she'd questioned how much he wanted her.

Chapter Eleven

Liam hadn't needed to open his eyes to know Colbie was awake. He swore the energy in the room shifted, and he smiled to himself. Damn, he was already so in tune with her, it amazed him.

"What are you smiling about?" Her quiet question surprised him. *I guess that smile wasn't as hidden as I thought it was.*

"I knew you were awake without opening my eyes. Sensing the shift in your consciousness made me feel connected to you in a very unique way, Spitfire." He opened his eyes to find her watching him cautiously, her brilliant blue eyes shining for the first time since she'd been injured. "You look like you're feeling better."

"I am, but to be honest, I'm afraid to move, and I really need to use the restroom." Her smile lit up the entire room.

Liam unfolded himself from the chair he'd been resting in and helped Colbie to her feet. When she laid her cheek against his chest, he felt like he'd just been hit with a sledge hammer. He wrapped his arms carefully around her and held her. For several minutes, neither of them moved or spoke. Until this moment, he'd never understood all the fuss about hugging. Some of the tension he'd been feeling the past several days drained away, leaving behind an odd sense of peace, despite the less than ideal circumstances.

When she finally shifted in his arms, he let her step back. The shy smile she gave him made Liam's heart leap. Very soon, she'd know how little need she'd have for *shy*. He and Bode would banish it from their relationship. He'd always known this would be more than a casual hook up. They'd always planned to bring her into their lives, but they hadn't planned for it to be as dramatic as it was turning out.

"If you want to take a shower, I think we could wrap your arm in plastic wrap to keep the dressing dry." Her hesitation was all the invitation he needed. "I'll shower with you, of course. I want to be sure you are steady on your feet. There's no need to add a concussion to the mix. And there's a bonus, too." He waggled his eyebrows at her in his best cartoon character imitation. "I'll get to see you naked—again."

"We both get to see her naked." Liam knew Bode had walked in behind her, but she hadn't noticed and let out a startled scream before spinning around so quickly her feet tangled beneath her. Colbie literally fell right into Bode's arms. "Damn, Storeen, you need to be more careful. Master Liam and I have plans for you later which do not include another visit to the local emergency room." She flushed before hurrying down the hall and the two men stood stock still, watching her retreat.

"I'm getting plastic wrap to put around her wound. We won't be able to stay in there long, but a brief lesson will be good for her." Liam made his way into the kitchen and returned a few seconds later with the wrap and a roll of bondage tape. When Bode raised a brow in question, Liam shrugged. "It will help secure the wrap and who knows what other uses we might find for it."

"A couple of bone shattering orgasms will help her

sleep later. She's wound pretty tight. Without the medication, I'm not sure she'd be sleeping at all." Bode might have been trying to pretend his motives were altruistic, but he wasn't fooling Liam. The man loved bondage and his eyes had brightened like a five-year-old who'd just gotten his first glimpse of the tree on Christmas morning when he'd seen the florescent pink tape.

"I agree. Gus said she's admitted having trouble sleeping at times." Liam hadn't been surprised. Considering everything she'd been through and the *fear of God* techniques the witness protection agents used, it was a wonder she slept at all.

"Let's go." Bode held up a bottle of shampoo and grinned. "I got this from the salon in the Forum Shops Spa. It's supposed to remove most of the coloring from her hair. They assumed she was using over-the-counter coloring kits and doing it herself, which means it will be easier to break it down."

In Liam's opinion, adding the small specialty shops behind the club had been pure genius. They specialized in all things kink. He'd wandered the small shops when they'd first arrived and marveled at the inventory and elaborate displays. Tobi and Gracie were gifted at marketing. It was easy to understand why they'd built such a successful business consulting for other clubs wanting to copy their idea.

"Did you make her an appointment? I want her waxed, and she should get any other treatments she wants as well." Liam was usually the one who took care of the spa appointments for any sub they'd dated, so he'd been surprised when Bode volunteered to make the arrangements. Nodding toward the master suite, he led the way down the hall.

"The appointment is made and Gracie helped choose the other services since Tobi was in Kyle's office. Her friend said she'd gone to talk to him about the nanny, but when I walked past the door on the way to the spa, I heard her screaming Kyle's name, so either their meeting went really well or it went south in a big way. Either way, I knew she wasn't going to walking out of there under her own steam for a while, so I graciously accepted Gracie's help."

They'd both stripped to the skin, stepped into the shower and went stock still. Colbie's sweet voice filled the air as she sang, "Leaving on a Jet Plane" by John Denver. Liam froze. Her voice was as good as any professional he'd ever heard; hell, she sang it better than John Denver and he'd written it. But it was the words that haunted him. It was one of the few songs from the 1970's he recognized. The lyrics about leaving sent a shiver up his spine. When she got to the part about returning, her voice broke.

"I don't fucking think so," Bode snarled as he stepped around Liam. She stood in the enormous shower wrapped in a towel. He was glad she hadn't started the water because he'd learned the hard way there were very few places in the large enclosure where you wouldn't be soaked in seconds. The damned thing had more showerheads than Home Depot.

BODE TILTED HER FACE up so her watery eyes met his and his frustration with her crumbled. She hadn't been planning to leave—she'd been trying to exorcise the thought.

"You sing like an angel, Storeen. We'll make sure we introduce you to Josie Morgan." Her eyes went wide, and she started shaking her head. He was surprised she'd recognized international pop superstar's, Josephine Alta, married name. "Shhh. She's a lovely woman and her husband, Colt is a friend of the Wests."

"Spitfire, how did you come upon your appreciation for oldies music?" Liam didn't want her worrying about performing in front of one of the biggest names in the music business. It was true they'd met Josie several times. Hell, they'd provided security for her on a number of occasions, even before they moved to the states.

"Mechanics at the tracks. I mean… they rarely listen to anything recorded after 1980. Well, unless it's country and even then, they are really persnickety."

"Persnickety?" Bode couldn't hold back his chuckle. "Damn, I don't think I've ever heard anyone under seventy use that word."

Liam had started wrapping her arm and he nodded in agreement. "I'm damned impressed with your singing, Spitfire."

"I learned early I could calm down the storms in the garage when things were going to hell if I sang. The craziness eased and everyone could focus on solving the problem rather than raging because the wrench they needed wasn't within reach."

Fucking hell, no wonder the pit crews like having her around. She was the calming breeze who cooled the hot heads and made the shop run like a well-oiled machine.

He studied her reaction when Liam pulled the bondage tape from the marble ledge behind him. He'd wondered if she would recognize it for what it was, and her soft gasp assured him she had. Goosebumps raced over her skin and her breathing hitched, but she didn't ask either of them what they planned with what Bode considered one of the best things ever invented. Hell, you could bind a sub in seconds without worrying about knots or chafing. He loved using it to "dress" a sub for a night at the club because unwrapping them always reminded him of opening a gift.

Once Liam finished securing the waterproof wrap over her wound, he stepped up to the control panel and began programming the shower. He shook his head and laughed.

"Who would have ever thought you'd have to push so many buttons to take a shower. Hell, I tried to use this shower when we first moved in and finally had to ask for help."

"I probably won't get to stay long enough to learn how to run it. I assume there's a locker room downstairs with showers, so I'll use that if you aren't here."

Bode wasn't sure she realized she'd said it aloud, but it didn't matter. They were going to derail that train of thought, right now. Framing her face with his hands, Bode forced her to look at him. He held her firmly in his grip—not harshly enough to bruise, but there would be no question who was in control.

"I know your case manager drilled those thoughts into your head, but we're telling you to banish them. Right fucking now because you aren't going anywhere."

"That's right, Spitfire. Even if MI6 got wind of this, which they won't if we can prevent it, we wouldn't let them take you. Despite what happened on the dock, you're safer here than anywhere they would send you."

Bode nodded. "And let me give you a tip. Don't insinuate that the Prairie Winds team can't protect you because you'll find out how dominant Kent and Kyle West really are." For the first time since they'd walked into Gus' office, Bode saw a flash of unease in her eyes. He found an odd sense of satisfaction knowing she wasn't comfortable with the prospect of being dominated by anyone besides the two men standing in front of her now.

"Give me the towel, Colbie." The heat in her gaze burned hot and bright. Sucking in a gulp of air, she slowly unwound the plush terry and set it in his outstretched hand. Anything he might have said halted on the tip of his tongue. The woman was perfection in the flesh. She might not be every man's ideal, but there wasn't a thing about her he'd change. Her breasts weren't huge, but they'd fit his hand perfectly. Dusky pink nipples drawn into tight points begged for decoration, and in time, he hoped to convince her to pierce them. Just imagining jewels dangling from small gold hoops sent a surge of blood to his cock.

Bode let his perusal slide sensuously down her torso and hoped she'd feel it as the visual caress it was. Liam moved behind her, and Bode watched her shiver when he leaned down to press a kiss where her shoulder and neck met. She shivered at the simple touch, and Bode made a mental note—it was the first of many sensitive points he hoped they'd discover. Liam's lilting voice whispered against her damp skin and her nipples puckered so tight, Bode knew the buds must ache for their touch.

"You are beautiful. I swear, God let his angels carve their likeness in ivory and then sent you to Earth. You're a precious gift. Lean back, baby. Let Master Liam help you. We're going to wash out that punk rocker color."

She'd leaned back against Liam's chest, but came up so quickly, he instinctively reached out to steady her. Cursing himself when she yelped in pain, Bode apologized, "I'm sorry, baby. Damn, I didn't think. I was worried about you falling. Are you okay?" He didn't think he'd grabbed her hard enough to open the sutures, but they'd need to check.

"Yes. Sorry I jumped, but if you wash out the red... well, my natural hair color is sort of distinctive." She pulled her lower lip between her teeth.

Watching her chew on the tender flesh made him want to push her against the smooth marble wall and cover her lips with his own. A blistering kiss would give her something else to focus on, but her fear needed to be addressed. Using his thumb to pull her battered lip from between her teeth, Bode shook his head and leaned down to press a chaste kiss against her swollen lips.

"Sweetheart, it's time to reclaim your life. They've already found you. It's time to stop hiding."

"It took me forever to recognize myself in the mirror. I'm not sure I can deal with another stranger staring back at me." Her voice cracked, and he knew she was nearing the edge.

It felt as if someone had reached into his chest and squeezed his heart. Bode wondered how anyone had the strength to endure witness protection. Those brave enough to try, lived every day in fear. The pain of having everything they knew and loved stripped from them was more than most people could endure. He hadn't considered the loneliness of having a stranger staring back from the mirror.

"Let us reintroduce you to the woman who knocked the wind out of us one rainy night in London. A woman who's been strong enough to start over and who can face whatever comes because we'll be standing behind her, ready to help in any way we can."

"Let's hope your confidence isn't misplaced." She'd spoken so softly, he might not have realized she'd said anything if he hadn't been watching her. Rather than issuing the reprimand on the tip of his tongue, he brushed his lips lightly over hers and helped her lean back against Liam. Giving the shampoo bottle a hefty squeeze, he lathered her short tresses and smiled when red-tinted water cascaded down in a waterfall of color before disappearing down the drain. Damn, he was glad to see the harsh color fading from her hair.

Ten minutes later, she stood in front of the mirror and burst out laughing, the sound bordering on hysteria. Bode stepped in front of her to block her image. He'd had enough experience with his sisters to recognize the coming meltdown.

"It's pink. It's fucking pink. I can't go out with pink hair. I look like a sun-faded flamingo. It's sticking out in every direction. I'll probably scare small children. The hell of it is, I have the bird legs to go with it."

Liam's eyes were wide with concern and Bode wanted to shake his head at his friend's confusion. Having a brother, ten years his junior, had done little to prepare Liam for Colbie's reaction. Bode, on the other hand, had lived through his sisters' numerous hair crises and knew how big a deal it could be. He'd made the mistake of laughing at his older sister's reaction to a bad haircut. She'd given him a *trim* of his own that night while he slept. He'd been forced to wear a hat for weeks, but he'd learned a damned valuable lesson.

"The ladies at the spa said it wouldn't all wash out the first time. And you have an appointment with them in a few days."

"A few days? Seriously? I can't help out in the garage with pink hair. I'll never hear the end of it. The caretaker is supposed to be back tonight, so I'd planned to meet him at the garage in the morning. He'll think I'm a flake. Hell, I'd think the same thing. I look like a hormone-crazed, middle school kid trying to get the attention of the boys who don't know what to do with their dicks."

Her voice had raised almost a full octave by the time she finished. Bode was startled by the outburst, but his surprise at her over-the-top response was eclipsed by the delighted female laughter from the door. Sharing a bathroom with an older and younger sister had rendered Bode immune to modesty, and he chuckled at Liam's mad scramble for a towel.

"Dammit, Tobi," Kent West's deep voice bellowed from the hall, "you can't just walk into someone else's house."

"I think I just proved I can. And holy hell, sister, those are a couple of fine fellas you have there. People don't surprise me very often, but I have to tell you, the closet hairdresser thing was a total shocker."

"Your Masters don't beat you enough, Tobi." Kent chuckled at Bode's observation as he led his wayward wife out of the master suite. Bode noticed Colbie hadn't made any effort to cover herself. She'd obviously become comfortable with her body during her time at Castle Masters. That ease would serve her well since they lived on the top floor of one of the country's most popular BDSM clubs. *And it'll make it much easier when she learns we want her bared to our touch—always.*

Chapter Twelve

TOBI FOUGHT THE URGE to roll her eyes at Kent's lecture about respecting other people's privacy. The man was the king of open doors. During the design and building phases of their new house, he'd continually threatened to remove all the interior doors from the plans. It had been their daughter who'd finally convinced him to leave them in place. Kodi had inherited her mother's impulsiveness, but she'd also learned how to sweetly manipulate people. The little imp had her dads wrapped around her finger since she'd taken her first breath and she used it, shamelessly.

Kameron's, Kodi's twin brother, calm was second only to his brilliance. He loved spending time with his grandfathers and if they weren't available, he could usually be found in Micah's office or the control center. Kent and Kyle had warned the staff it didn't matter how helpful he was, he had to be out of the building a full hour before the club opened. Seemed her open-minded husbands didn't feel those relaxed views should apply to their elementary school aged son.

"I called out several times and no one answered. I thought the men were working and when I heard Colbie's squeal, I ran to help." She paused long enough to lean against him and bat her eyes in an overly dramatic gesture. "You know how I am. Always rushing in where angels fear to tread. I'm an angel of mercy. Yes, indeed, Florence Nightingale has nothing on me."

"That you are, baby, that you are. The question is how can we manage it so you don't see and comment on other men's assets?" Dozens of ideas streamed through her mind, but Colbie and her men chose that moment to walk into the room. She'd asked Kent to follow her upstairs to check on Colbie when he'd surprised her by arriving home several hours before she'd expected him. *If I'd known he was so close, I'd have held out for a two-fer.*

"Colbie, I'm so happy to see you're feeling better. I wanted to check in before Kent and I went home." She let her gaze flick to Liam and Bode and grinned. "I'd say I'm sorry for barging in, but it would be a lie." To her relief, Colbie leaned her head back and laughed.

"I'd have never believed it, anyway. All things considered, I doubt Liam and Bode are the first naked men you've ever seen. I would imagine living in a penthouse over a kink club is very enlightening."

Tobi got the distinct impression there was a story behind Colbie's comment and she was looking forward to learning more about her new friend.

"For what it's worth, I think your hair is funky and cool. But, I sure hope Kodi doesn't see it or I'm sure she'll want to color hers, too. It will have to be some bizarre fusion of contrasting colors. She's been redesigning our displays because we aren't… and I quote, *using hues to draw the eye in the most efficient way.* Can you believe that nonsense? Some demon gave her a color wheel and put a design app on her iPad. When I find out who is responsible, I'm unleashing the hounds of hell on them. Or maybe I'll just send her to their house to help them redecorate."

"I'd like to say Tobi isn't usually like this," Kent shook

his head and sighed, "but you all know better. Come on, before you get into any more trouble. You've seen for yourself Colbie is fine, and I need to take the edge off before we hit the club tonight, or I'll have you stripped and bent over in the reception area. I'll never last until the scene Kyle has planned." Tobi's eyes widened and a grin spread over her face.

"Scene, huh?" He shrugged as if he hadn't just spilled the beans. Grabbing his hand, she waved at Colbie and tugged on his arm until he started moving toward the elevator. She could only imagine how ridiculous they looked, her five-foot-nothing-self towing Kent along behind her like an overgrown pull toy. Giving the trio watching them one last wave as the elevator doors slid closed, Tobi grinned. "Later. Places to go, Masters to do."

COLBIE WATCHED THE elevators doors close, then burst out laughing. For the first time in over a year, she allowed herself to become lost in the moment, just absorbing the joy she'd felt watching Tobi's antics. When she finally regained a semblance of self-control, she saw Bode and Liam smiling at her.

"That's just about the sweetest sound I've ever heard. One I hope we get to hear more often in the future." Liam's words calmed her in a way she hadn't expected. She wasn't sure if it was the compliment or the fact he'd alluded to them having a future together.

Bode pushed away from the counter where he'd been leaning and pulled her close. "We had planned to do a walk-through downstairs this evening, but if you don't get some rest, we'll table it until tomorrow night."

"So, if I don't take a nap, I don't get to go to the party?" She'd been joking, but Bode's glare told her he hadn't seen the humor in her remark.

"It's our responsibility as your Doms to take care of you. Everything we do will be to that end." The shift in his voice and body language gave Colbie her first real glimpse of Master Bode. She'd seen a similar change in Deacon and had marveled at the marked difference between the man who was her godfather and the Master at the club. She suspected there would be a similar difference between the gentle lover she'd just showered with and the Master she was seeing now.

Liam shifted so he was close enough she could feel the heat from his arm against her own. She suspected those differences would be more understated in Liam. If he could, he'd use charm to dominate. When he slid the backs of his fingers down the side of her cheek, the touch brought her back to the moment.

"There will be times our commands won't set well with you. Times when you feel we're being overly restrictive or we're treating you like a child. But I want to assure you, we're well aware you aren't a child." The gleam in his eyes said he was remembering their shower. "We won't always explain our reasoning. There are times when the element of surprise will add to your pleasure. As we begin, we'll focus on learning about each other."

Colbie realized she had to learn about two people and they only had to learn about one. "I want to point out I'll have two people to become familiar with. Two people to try to please. What happens if you give me conflicting instructions? Is one of you in charge over the other?" Colbie felt herself winding up and knew she was headed for a crash. *Damn, they might be right about resting.*

Liam pushed his fingers through her hair so that the warmth of his palm pressed against her cheek. "We'll use this as a teachable moment, Spitfire. You are dangerously close to crashing, so we'll table this discussion until later. But the short answer to your question is, no. Neither of us is *in charge* of the other, and it will never be your job to keep the peace between us. Those discussions will be between Bode and myself."

She felt blindsided as a crashing wave of exhaustion hit her full force. *Is it from the injury or a reaction to the stress of the entire episode?* Sleeping didn't hold any appeal because every time she closed her eyes the entire scene on the dock replayed itself. Swaying on her feet, Colbie shook her head trying to clear the cobwebs. The sudden sensation of falling came to an abrupt halt, and she realized she was being cradled in someone's arms. *Maybe I could sleep if you just held me? Would you do it if I begged? I don't want to be that scared ever again.*

LIAM WATCHED HER sway unsteadily on her feet before her eyes rolled back. He'd already been reaching for her when her knees folded out from under her, and she dropped into his waiting arms. Bode had growled a litany of curses as he led the way to the bedroom. He'd already tossed the comforter onto a nearby chair and was pulling back the covers when her slurred words made them both freeze.

"Did she just say she wants to be held, so she can sleep?" Bode blinked at him as if he couldn't believe he'd heard it right.

"Yes," Liam grinned. "Knowing her subconscious is seeking comfort in our arms gives me a tremendous amount of hope. Text Kyle that we'll be busy the rest of the day." The first time she was naked in bed, she needed to be between them. Later they'd make sure they had one-on-one time with her. But for now—presenting a united front was in all their best interests. Sliding between the sheets a few seconds later, Liam cursed when Colbie wiggled her bare ass against his aching cock.

"Fuck me. Baby, you're playing with fire. Stop wiggling that sweet ass of yours and sleep. I promise we'll take care of that ache after you've gotten some rest." Liam wasn't sure whether or not she'd heard him because she didn't settle. Bode moved closer and began caressing the side of her face while whispering soothing words, and their sweet sub quieted immediately. As her breathing slowed, he felt her body go lax against his own.

"Damn, I hadn't realized how tense she was until it drained away."

"It was like watching a balloon deflate. Constantly being on your guard would be exhausting. No one should have to live like that." Bode moved closer, so she'd wake up sheltered between them. Liam appreciated the gesture and hoped, on some level, she knew they were as close as they could be without being inside her. *And that's going to happen sooner rather than later if I don't get my damned cock to take it down a notch or ten.—*

Closing his eyes, Liam let himself float in the sweet space where everything is fuzzy before sleep pulled him under. If he fell into a deep sleep now, he'd be up all night, and he would likely keep Colbie up as well. He mentally reviewed the plans they'd made for her first trip to the club. Their walk-through had already been carefully mapped out. He and Bode were both looking forward to seeing if any of her hard or soft limits had changed since she'd filled out the club's paperwork a year ago.

Kyle had encouraged her to transfer her membership from Castle Masters. When Liam asked if he'd been hoping they'd be able to better monitor her if she was close, the man had nodded. But then his expression had sobered and he'd shaken his head. "I should have known she was too much like Tobi for it to work."

Kent had burst out laughing. "I keep telling him that he must have fucked up with a petite blonde in a previous life and this is karma, but he won't listen to me."

Kyle's response had come so quickly, Liam knew it was a conversation they'd had before. "Fuck you. Having you for twin should have paid every karma debt I had." Remembering the conversation made Liam smile. He'd never worked with a team whose members were as close as the ones here at Prairie Winds.

"Don't be a baby. Suck it up and push the pain back, Colbie." Colbie's whimper brought him back from his musings, and he felt her rocking against him. He looked over her shoulder to see Bode frowning.

"Storeen, if you are in pain, you need to tell us. Pain inhibits healing. I swear, we're going to have a serious talk about the importance of asking for help."

Liam moved just far enough he could ease her onto her back. Looking down into her drawn features, he gave her a look he hoped conveyed his frustration. Without saying a word, he got up and padded naked into the kitchen where he'd left her medications. Returning with an over-the-counter pain reliever and a glass of water, he wasn't surprised to see her sitting up, waiting. She didn't argue when he held out two tablets.

"Thank you. For what it's worth, I slept better than I have in a long time."

"Why haven't you been sleeping, Colbie?" Liam hadn't planned to have this discussion until after their meeting with the Wests tomorrow morning, but she'd given him an opening, and he was going to take it. He didn't like the way her shoulders slumped or how they seemed to fold inward as if she was trying to make herself invisible.

"Things in my apartment have been moved lately. Not from the team coming in and looking around, they were always careful. This was different."

Liam was speechless and from the gobsmacked look on Bode's face, he was equally surprised. "Wait. You knew we were coming in and looking for bugs?"

"I didn't know it was you, specifically," she shrugged and then winced, "but I knew Kent and Kyle weren't happy I wasn't where they could watch me closer. It only made sense they'd snoop."

Bode leaned his head back and laughed as Liam shook his head. They should have known she wasn't naïve enough to believe the Wests had accepted her decision to move over the garage. She looked up, and he was relieved to see some of the pain had started to fade from her eyes.

"I wasn't able to prove it until a few months ago. I always aligned things so perfectly, I was sure whoever they sent would leave something slightly askew." As she took a steadying breath, Liam realized how much they'd underestimated her. "But nothing ever seemed out of place... yet, I could sense someone else had been in the space. Then, I got lucky. The cereal box I kept money in was set back too far on the shelf. All the money was still there, but someone was careless when they replaced it."

"God bless it, I warned them." Bode's outburst made her grin.

"I knew it. You were the ones who were so careful,

right? And then for some reason someone else was assigned babysitting duty and got sloppy." Neither of them bothered to respond because there was little doubt she'd slide the next piece of the puzzle into place quickly, and he wasn't disappointed.

"Holy shit. You saw the pictures on my refrigerator. That's why you call me Spitfire." Liam nodded and he was shocked to see her eyes went glassy with tears. "That's why you bought it, isn't it? The car I was working on, you bought it because of the pictures, didn't you?" He nodded, and she closed her eyes. "That's the nicest thing anyone has ever done for me." When he looked at Bode for help, his friend chuckled at his discomfort.

"That car was a heap when he found it. You wouldn't believe how much money he's invested in that little death trap. Hell, his accountant almost had a stroke."

"Fuck him. He probably doesn't even know how to drive." Softening his voice, he returned his attention to Colbie, giving her a small smile. "It's a sweet little car, and I hoped it would give me an 'in' when we were finally able to meet face to face again."

"Why would you spend that much money on a woman you dropped off at your headquarters and walked away from? You ushered me into that room and couldn't get away from me fast enough. And… and you never looked back." Her voice broke. Liam felt shame wash over him.

"Christ, I'm going to wring his fucking neck." Bode had been pissed at their supervisor's demand they stand down, and Liam had spent the rest of the night acting as the peacemaker. But now, knowing how hurt she'd been by their actions, he felt two inches tall. "We might have walked out of the room, but we didn't abandon you. Our supervisor was calling the shots that night, and while I understood what he was trying to do, I also knew it wasn't going to work. I swear I'd fly to London and put a boot in his ass if I thought it would take away the pain I see in your eyes."

"I know it shouldn't, but that really does make me feel better. I'll admit, I've thought about hurting him myself... maybe detaching an appendage or two. He's what I like to call a reverse snob. He hated me on sight because of my social position. A social position I didn't earn or want, by the way. Although amputating a part I doubt he's been able to use for years would probably have been futile."

Liam chuckled and raised a brow, thoroughly surprised at her response. "Master Bode, did you know our sub was a blood-thirsty, little wench?"

"No, but I like it." Bode's eyes blazed with desire, and Liam knew it was time to begin. Using the tip of his finger, Liam circled her areola, watching it pucker. Colbie gasped, her eyes going wide.

"Did you forget you were naked, Spitfire?"

"Yes." He gave her nipple a quick pinch and she quickly corrected her mistake. "Yes, Sir, I had forgotten." She might not be an experienced submissive, but she had been trained in one of the world's most respected clubs. It impressed him how quickly she'd amended her response.

"Good girl." She flushed at his words, and he shifted closer. Not everyone had been convinced she was submissive, but Liam and Bode had known from the moment they first saw her. She'd become theirs the night they'd met—she just hadn't known it.

Chapter Thirteen

Bode moved down the bed and tapped the inside of her thigh with his finger. She opened her legs without being told, and he rewarded her with a string of kisses along her smooth skin. The taut muscles twitched beneath his lips in response, and he inhaled the heady smell of her arousal.

"Is your pussy wet, baby?" Twirling his fingers through the blonde curls covering her mound, Bode could hardly wait for her spa appointment; having her completely bare was going to be a treat for all of them.

"Yes, Sir." He was pleased she'd remembered how to address him properly and twirled his tongue lazily through her wet folds as a reward. She tried to arch her back, but Liam had anticipated the move and held her in place with his palm spanning her chest. The contrast of Liam's tanned skin against Colbie's ivory perfection was as erotic as anything he'd ever seen. Her rose colored nipples peeking from between Liam's fingers begged for attention.

Watching Liam lean down and suck first one, then the other bud tested Bode's control. One of the perks of ménage was having a front row seat to a woman's pleasure, it didn't matter that Liam was the one providing it.

Bode had always enjoyed watching others, often preferring it to participating. Liam had a similar voyeuristic side, making their partnership even stronger, but in the end, it was all about pushing the boundaries of the woman between them. Their number one priority was her pleasure.

"Open for me, baby. Let me give you a preview of what's to come." Her legs were moving before he'd stopped speaking. He knew her body had responded before her quick mind had a chance to process the words. *Perfect.* "God, you smell amazing." Using his fingers to open her fully to his view, he flicked his tongue over her clit, making it come fully out from under its hood. There would be no hiding for that sweet spot. "Let's see how quickly I can take you over the edge, shall we?"

Bode didn't give her an opportunity to answer before sealing his lips over the sensitive bundle of nerves and slipping his middle finger into her tight sheath. Her scream was music to his ears and the pulsing of her vaginal muscles made him long to be buried so deep in her, they both forgot their own names. Her release streamed over his fingers, the sweet taste coating his tongue and feeding his own pleasure. Ordinarily, they'd insist she come at least twice before they fucked her, but they didn't want to tire her before their walkthrough at the club. *And I hope like hell this gives her something to look forward to.*

An hour later, Bode and Liam set the last platter on the table as Colbie walked into the room. She'd washed her hair again, and he was pleased to see almost all traces of the residual pink had disappeared. The light touches of makeup she wore enhanced her porcelain features. Bode wondered what she would say if he told her she reminded him of the dolls lining the shelves of his grandmother's living room.

Liam broke the silence when he held out his hand and called her to his side. "Come, Spitfire. Let me look at you." She turned when he twirled his fingers and a wash of pink colored her cheeks. "You're beautiful. This dress suits you and the color matches your eyes perfectly." When she tried to duck her head, Liam shook his head; Bode knew what was coming.

Bode always considered Liam at a disadvantage because he didn't grow up with sisters. His friend didn't always understand the complicated way women's minds worked. Bode knew some women were embarrassed by compliments. Even the ones who loved the praise would often blush furiously, no matter how subtle the remark. He leaned against the counter and watched the interplay between Liam and Colbie, schooling his amusement—another skill he'd learned early on.

"Colbie, when we tell you you're beautiful, we expect you to acknowledge the compliment. It may not be easy at first, but I promise you, it will get easier and eventually you'll believe us." She nodded and offered a thank you that was half-assed, at best. When Liam looked up, Bode shook his head. *Choose your battles, buddy. We'll have ample opportunities to push her.*

COLBIE COULD FEEL the energy of the club before the elevator doors had even begun opening. It pulsed up the shaft, seeping into the small space, electrifying her nerve endings. She resisted bouncing on the balls of her feet, but it was a struggle. When the doors slid apart, the music's thumping bass pounded against her chest and assaulted her ears. She wasn't accustomed to music this loud because Deacon had always considered it uncivilized.

Cringing as Bode and Liam led her past a large speaker, she saw Liam cast a disgruntled look at the black box. *Yes, siree. Leveling a look at an inanimate object is going to be really effective.* She pulled her hand from Bode's to cover her arm when the vibrations made it feel like someone was thumping their fingers directly over the injury. When his gaze followed her movements, he frowned and quickened his pace until she was practically running to keep up.

Kent stepped in front of them and frowned. "Where's the fire?"

"We walked by the speakers and it's so fucking loud, the vibrations hurt Colbie's arm." Bode's frustrated tone and Kent's scrutiny made Colbie want to disappear into the woodwork.

"Sorry, sweetie." Kent picked up her hand and pressed a kiss to the back. "I just got here and the early crew likes to get everybody wound up. I'll take care of it. In the meantime, Kirk and Brian are waiting for you at the first aid station." She tried to ask him what they wanted, but he was already stomping toward the bar.

Liam must have sensed her confusion because he leaned close and spoke against the shell of her ear as they walked out of the din of the main room. "They wanted us to bring you into their clinic, but the entire team objected, so they've agreed to check you here." She was instantly pissed. No one had told her the doctors had called nor had they given her the option of making alternate arrangements. Her feet stopped moving, and both men cursed when they literally lifted her off the ground with their forward momentum.

"What the fuck, Colbie? Damn it, did we hurt you?" Oh yeah, they'd hurt her all right, but not in the way they were thinking.

"The *team* decided? Feathers! What made you think it was okay to exclude me from this discussion? What am I, a frick-fracking toddler who can't make her own decisions? Holy Christmas and Blessed Easter, I'll have you know I'm perfectly capable of making my own medical decisions... hell, I'm actually considered of sound mind in most circles. Okay, maybe not most, but certainly some circles." Before she could stop herself, she stomped her foot, a habit she'd had since childhood when she'd been holding on to her temper by a fraying thread.

Cackling laughter sounded from her left and she swiveled to see who'd been listening to her tirade. The petite blonde standing between two giants had eyes the color of blue crystal, reminding her of the sparkling water of the Caribbean Sea.

"I like her. And she's right, you know. Self-determination is a basic human right in almost every country in the world, including this one."

The man on her right shook his head and slid his hand under her long curls. Colbie watched her hair tighten as he tilted her face up to his. "Be careful, Pet, Masters Liam and Bode might not appreciate your lesson in diplomatic relations."

Colbie remembered hearing that one of the women on the Prairie Winds team had been held at gun point in an American Embassy before being rescued by Navy SEALs. Colbie had never met her, but she'd read several of her articles on how to read body language.

"But we're in the reception area, so I'm allowed to speak freely." She looked down at the threshold Colbie had just crossed and smiled. "Colbie is also in the lobby." Mischief danced in her eyes as she pointed to the floor. "See? *This* is why it's important to teach geography in school. Do you know that very few curriculums include geography anymore?"

"And *this*, sweet cheeks, is why no one lets Suzie play with their children. Our sweet daughter is being penalized because her mama is a hot mess." The man standing on her left grinned, the orneriness absolutely oozed from him.

"I suppose I should be grateful you still consider me *hot*." A flash of pain showed itself in the woman's eyes, but it was gone so quickly, Colbie wondered if it had been her imagination. The woman held out her hand, "Hi, I'm Jen McCall. It's nice to meet you. These two handsome fellas are my husbands, Sam and Sage." She'd waved her hand right and then left, telling Colbie which one was which. "Sage and I were in the helicopter the day that ass ant shot at you." *Ass ant? What the hell does that mean?*

Liam chuckled from her side, "Jen has a unique way of blending phrases. She's under the mistaken impression it keeps her Masters from knowing she's cursing."

Colbie shook hands and thanked her for her help, but Jen waved her off. "I'm just sorry we didn't catch the fuc...jerk." Jen glanced between the men flanking here and shrugged, obviously trying to apologize for the near slip. "But once the boat went under the tree canopy we were screwed... and not in a good way. Now I see why Kyle is so anal about keeping the bank around the dock clear."

"Well, sweetness, the women at Prairie Winds are trouble magnets, and we need every advantage we can get to hold the forces of evil at bay." Kyle West's smooth voice came from behind her, and Colbie turned to see genuine affection in his eyes. It was obvious the man who usually seemed so stern, had a soft spot for the pretty blonde. "Good evening, Colbie. I'd like to apologize for the loud music. I'm certain it didn't occur to the staff it might cause you pain."

"It didn't occur to me either. I'm fine, please don't be

angry with them." Colbie stilled when she realized it was the first time in almost a year she'd fallen back into her old pattern of apologizing and worrying about someone's anger. She'd promised herself she would never become the simpering debutante her parents had wanted her to be, but it had been a daily battle. Some days, she'd been more successful than others.

Her mother had never understood her dislike of all the pomp and circumstance associated with their social position and had done everything in her power to berate her daughter into compliance. In many ways, her new life had been liberating and the thought of becoming anything resembling the Stepford daughter her mother had wanted made her want to jump off a bridge. *God damn it, I forgot I was mad.*

Jen gave her a knowing smile, and Colbie felt some of her frustration fade. "I'd like to speak with Colbie for a minute while you all-knowing and powerful Masters plot against us poor defenseless subs." Jen batted her lashes at the men surrounding them, and Colbie sucked in a breath at the brazen display. Good Lord, somewhere, a melodrama was missing their heroine.

"It's a miracle you didn't get struck by lightning with that nonsense, sweet cheeks." Sage shook his head and kissed her before pointing to the other side of the room. "Stay where we can keep an eye on you. I don't want weapons changing hands or anything. God only knows what you could cook up if you were out of sight."

Jen stood with her back to the men facing the corner and pulled Colbie into a similar position. "Okay, spill. What were you so pissed about? Holy shizam, sister, it was coming off you in waves."

Colbie told the other woman about the team making

medical decisions for her without even consulting her and how angry she'd been when she'd found out. She didn't hold back, and Jen grinned at her brutal honesty. When she finally took a deep breath, Jen turned and gave her a quick hug.

"Let all that anger sink lower and lower until it all seeps into the floor, girlfriend. If you get all wound up about the little things... and trust me, when dealing with two dominant men, this is a little thing, you'll drive yourself insane. You have to choose your battles."

When Colbie started to argue she should have been consulted, Jen held up her hand. "I get it, I really do. But ask yourself this, would you have done anything differently?" Colbie took a deep breath and when her shoulders slumped, Jen chuckled. "Damn, I really do understand that frustration. Just remember, their hearts are in the right place, even if they have their heads up their asses. And heaven knows that happens a lot."

Colbie rolled her shoulders, trying to push the last of the frustration out of her muscles. The pinch of pain was a small price to pay for the calm it brought to her soul.

"Thank you. I would have really messed things up if you hadn't stepped in. I just... well, I hope you don't get into too much trouble."

The flash of pain she'd seen in Jen's eyes reappeared for a heartbeat, but was quickly masked.

"Don't worry. My Masters are busy men, I'll be surprised if they even remember I'm here."

Chapter Fourteen

Bode was glad he and Sam had moved close enough to overhear Jen's conversation with Colbie. He made a mental note to thank Jen for her help and let her know how grateful he was she'd headed off the runaway train of emotion Colbie had been riding when they entered the club's reception area. Neither of the women had noticed the ornately framed mirror hanging nearby, letting the Doms monitor their facial expressions, something he found particularly helpful with Colbie. She was so new to the lifestyle, he needed every available piece of information.

Oddly enough, it was Sam who'd learned the most from watching Jen and Colbie's reflections. They might have missed the faint thread of pain in her voice, but the sadness in her eyes was unmistakable. Jen masked her unhappiness quickly, but not before Sam caught it. Bode watched his friend's expression change from loving indulgence to concern in the blink of an eye. Sam turned and gave his brother a quick hand signal that immediately brought Sage to his side. The silent communication that passed between the brothers had them both frowning as they turned to lead Jen from the room.

Sam gave her ass a quick swat. "Pet, we're going to have a long conversation about your lagging communication skills." Bode watched as Jen seemed to shut down emotionally, and he wondered how long it would take the

McCalls to break through whatever wall she was silently erecting. He knew the three of them had worked almost continuously since their daughter had been born and wondered if their relentless schedules weren't contributing to Jen's unhappiness.

"She looks sad... she tries to hide it, but it's not hard to see if you're watching." Colbie's gentle voice brought him back to the present, and he pulled her into his arms.

"Yes, she does and her Masters are going to find out what's going on and fix it. They adore her. I know they'll do everything they can to give her whatever she needs." And that was the absolute truth. Bode had seen the way both men looked at their lovely wife. They loved her, but more importantly, they respected her as a teammate. The sudden insight that observation gave him into Colbie's earlier anger brought him up short. Before he and Liam led her into the first aid room, Bode turned her so she faced them both.

"Storeen, I want to apologize." He hated seeing her eyes widen in surprise; the fact her Doms could make and admit to a mistake shouldn't be a surprise. Some Doms didn't believe in any show of weakness, but Bode didn't feel that was realistic. In the end, if a submissive didn't believe his or her Dominant would apologize when they were wrong, any love and respect between them would crack and eventually fall apart. "We should have consulted you about the appointment. We've asked you to trust us, but we didn't offer you the same consideration."

Liam nodded in agreement. "We've only just started on this journey together, Spitfire, but I promise you we only had your best interests at heart."

"I know, I'm sorry if I overreacted." Colbie's eyes looked glassy with unshed tears, but she valiantly held them back. "Jen asked me if I would have done it differently, and I know I wouldn't have wanted to go. So…" She let the rest of the thought hang in the air, and he breathed a silent sigh of relief. Admitting she would have acted in her own best interest was a huge relief. He'd seen submissives deliberately compromise their safety just to prove to the Doms they could.

Brilliant women didn't submit easily, but when they did, it was the sweetest gift in the world because the Dom knew it was a carefully considered decision. Colbie had been making her own decisions for the past year; they'd known it wasn't going to be easy for her to relinquish control. *Well, she thinks she's been making independent decisions.* The entire team had kept close tabs on her, and Gus had kept them informed, but if she'd put that last piece of the puzzle together, she had yet to mention it.

Liam took one of her hands and held it between his own. "It pleases me that you would have made the same decision, but I agree with Bode, we should have discussed it with you. Trust is earned through shared experiences and over time. The only experience you had with us before a few days ago involved us handing you over at MI6 Headquarters and walking out the door. You had no way to know we'd watched you for hours—completely enthralled with your courage and resolve. I swear on all things holy, it took every ounce of my self-control to not march back in that room, throw you over my shoulder and make a break for it." Liam might give outsiders the impression he was all about propriety, but Bode knew that wasn't who he was at his core.

The door beside them opened and Regi, the Wests' former office manager stuck her head out. "My Masters are waiting. They'll take their frustration out on me during our scene later, so I'd appreciate it if you'd get your happy fannies in here."

Bode heard Kirk growl, "Anoshi, that's ten."

She winced before continuing, "See? Doc and Happy have left the building leaving Grumpy and Grouchy here to torture me." Turning her attention to Colbie, the little pixie grinned. "Grumpy Doc has a new violet wand, and I'd rather he didn't use it on my pink bits, so if you'd cut the chit-chat, I'd appreciate it." Much to his relief, Colbie giggled and nodded before following Regi into the best equipped club infirmary Bode had ever seen. Hell, a lot of hospital emergency rooms weren't as state-of-the art as the area the Wests humbly referred to as a first aid station.

Kirk greeted them, and Bode noticed Brian seated in the exam room, typing furiously on his laptop. "Brian is trying to connect to our clinic, but isn't having any luck. Micah and Phoenix can't get in either, which means we've probably got a serious security breach." Bode wasn't sure which was louder, Colbie's gasp or Brian's cursing from a few yards away. The computer problem might be a coincidence, but Bode doubted it.

"Colbie, come in here, sweetie. I want to take a look at your arm." Brian looked up and frowned when he and Liam followed her in. "Sorry guys, you'll have to wait outside. I was trying to print off the forms for Colbie to sign allowing you to be here but since I can't get into the system…"

"What? We were in the E.R. with her." Bode didn't understand why is Brian was being a stickler for the rules now.

"Colbie?" Kirk stepped forward in an obvious attempt to mediate, and Bode was grateful to have an advocate.

She looked at Kirk and smiled. "I'd like for them to

stay. I want them to know I'm okay. Or they're never going to play with me." Every man in the room froze, it was Regi who broke the spell with a soft chuckle.

"Oh, yes. She is going to fit in here just fine." Regi stepped up to Colbie and gave her a high-five.

Bode felt like the weight of the world had just been lifted from his shoulders. She'd said when and not if; the certainty that he'd heard in her tone flooded him with relief. Somewhere deep in his subconscious, he'd still been worried she wouldn't trust them to keep her safe and take off.

"Damn, I wish I didn't have to work on your spa day. I hear it's shaping up to be a great party."

Regi gave Kirk a hopeful look and he shook his head. "Not a chance in hell, Anoshi. You are gas to Tobi's fire. Besides, how would we ever function without you?"

Colbie looked at Kirk and tilted her head to the side in a move which reminded Bode how young she was. It was easy to forget because she'd been through so much.

"What does Anoshi mean? I've heard you call her that twice and I'm curious." Her eyes suddenly went wide and she looked between Bode and Liam. *"Feathers.* Am I allowed to ask questions here? I mean… we aren't really in the club's main areas even though we're in the building. But then we live in the building, and if I can't ask questions anywhere in the whole place, I'm really screwed and like Jen said… not it a good way."

Brian and Kirk were both chuckling and Regi's eyes were wide in surprise, but she wasn't speechless for long. "Wow. Are you and Tobi long lost sisters or something?"

Kirk stepped forward up to the exam table where Colbie sat and carefully removed the bandage covering her wound. *"Anoshi* is Navajo for *my love*. My lovely wife is a sassy sub and she deserved a unique name. I also wanted to honor my ancestors because she is a precious gift they sent to me."

Ten minutes later the two doctors had assured them Colbie's arm was healing perfectly, and they were nearing the entrance to the main club room. When they paused, she looked at them in question when Bode pushed her gently against the wood paneled wall. Liam pulled a black velvet bag from his pocket and smiled down at her. "We can't have you walking around the club without something to keep the predators at bay."

"Predators?" She might have phrased the word as a question, but Bode knew she'd spent enough time at Castle Masters to know exactly what Liam had been referring to.

"Yes, Pet. We don't plan to let you out of our sight, but we won't take any chances, either."

Bode stood shoulder to shoulder with Liam as he reached forward to trace his fingers down the side of her face. He let a ghost of a smile tip up the corners of his lips and sighed at the shift in her body language. Bode could see the anticipation in her eyes, she was looking forward to wearing a sign of their ownership. "This is a temporary collar, Colbie. This is just something to let other Doms know you are not available."

She nodded her understanding, but quickly corrected her mistake. "I understand. Thank you for thinking of my safety, Sir." Bode was pleased she'd already been introduced to the basics of protocol—it was a relief to know she was much less likely to make a serious error which would subject her to a public punishment. He'd seen it happen to newbie subs before, and it was usually the last time anyone ever saw them at the club. He also heard the note of disappointment in her voice and shook his head.

"I won't deny your safety is an issue, but I assure you that's not the only reason we want you wearing a temporary collar. We may share, but we only share with each other."

"You are ours, Pet. It would be bad form to get into an altercation if another Dom decided to test our resolve." Liam's words soothed something deep inside her, and she let a small spark of hope flair. Maybe she'd finally found a place she could call home… at least for a while.

"It's exquisite," Colbie gasped when Liam pulled a sapphire and diamond necklace from the velvet bag. She wasn't sure what she'd been expecting, but it certainly hadn't been the beautiful piece of jewelry he was holding in his hand.

"We're glad you like it. We wanted something you could wear everywhere without drawing unwanted attention from those outside the lifestyle." The snick of the clasp sent a shiver up her spine and she shuddered. Liam smiled down at her in satisfaction. "This will also remind you that your submission belongs to us. The weight laying against your feminine neck a constant reminder you are cherished and owned.

EMOTIONS RIOTING, COLBIE was grateful they'd given her a minute to pull herself together before opening the door to the main room. Her hand came up to caress the jewels and both men smiled at her indulgently. Stepping over the threshold, she was assailed by the sights and sounds of the club. It had been so long since she'd been inside a kink club, it all seemed new again. The Prairie Winds Club was larger than Deacon's Castle Masters in London, the décor entirely different, but the pulsing energy of sexual desire radiating all around her was unmistakable.

Her godfather had never let her explore the darker recesses of his facility, restricting her to the most public areas where he and his staff could monitor her every move. It had annoyed her at the time, but now she realized, he'd had her best interests at heart and was grateful for his caution. Even though the sounds and smells were familiar, Colbie felt she was experiencing everything for the first time, thanks to the men standing beside her. Liam gave her hand a quick squeeze to get her attention, and she looked up at him in question.

"Ordinarily, subs aren't allowed to gawk around the club. There are Doms who will take offense if you look at them directly."

"It's considered a challenge to their authority, and they'll enjoy taking you down a peg or two." Colbie had the feeling Bode was grossly understating the trouble she could find herself in, but she wasn't going to tempt fate by asking.

"Since this is your first visit to the club, we won't leave your side. It will be obvious to anyone watching you're new and most will make some allowance for that. But you'd do well to look carefully tonight because things will be different after this." Liam pulled her into his arms and pressed a kiss to the top of her head. "Breathe, Spitfire. If you hold your breath every time we're explaining something about the club, you're going to pass out before we've seen anything interesting."

Colbie sucked in a deep breath and felt some of the tension drain away. Damn it, she knew these rules. Why was she behaving like a complete novice? *Because Liam and Bode are important.* Admitting how much she wanted to please them was startling, but it didn't feel like a threat to her independence as she'd feared it might.

"Good evening. I'm happy to see you made it." Tobi's southern twang was endearing, and Colbie turned to see the feisty blonde standing between Kent and Kyle. The dress the other woman wore, if you could call it a dress, was so sheer she might as well have been nude. Her jeweled nipple clamps sparkled in the dim light. *Feathers. They'd probably be blinding under bright light.* Colbie was confused by the woman's subdued behavior, and it must have shown in her expression because Kent laughed.

"It's almost scary, isn't it?" When she didn't respond, he grinned. "When Tobi is quiet, it throws people off. It's like that strange calm before a violent storm. Spooky."

Colbie worked hard to school her expression. She didn't want to hurt her new friend's feelings by laughing at her husband's ridiculous nonsense. Tobi rolled her eyes and grinned.

"It's okay, you can laugh at him. I know it's weird when I'm quiet, but I'm trying to rack up some grace points before our scene tonight. And to be honest, I'm so far in the hole in the points tally, dead even would be a blessing and probably a miracle."

"Pet, don't set yourself up for failure." Kyle's lips twitched. Colbie found herself letting out a breath she hadn't even realized she was holding. Knowing the men weren't actually angry with Tobi was a huge relief. Some of the Doms at Deacon's club had been ruthless, and the one time she'd snuck into the dungeon, she'd been so frightened, she hadn't ever wanted to go back. Colbie had nightmares about the crack of a whip for months. *Served me right for defying Deacon.* She shuddered, earning concerned frowns from the Doms around her.

Tobi seemed oblivious to the shift in the mood. In what Colbie suspected was typical Tobi fashion, the other woman continued as if Kyle hadn't spoken.

"It's not fair, you know. I was chatting with Lilly. She'll be joining us for our spa day, which has been changed to tomorrow by the way. That takes Jen out because she'll be playing war games with the boys, but maybe if she kills all her paper dolls, they'll let her out of class early. Anyway, Gracie and I were making some special snacks for tomorrow, and I got distracted." She waved her hand in the air when Kent snorted a laugh. "I know. I know. It's hard to believe, but it happens." Colbie watched as both Kent and Kyle gaped at their wife, the expressions so filled with utter disbelief it made her wonder about the stories behind those looks.

"Anyway, the bacon might have gotten a little crispy before we noticed the smoke." *Smoke? Oh boy.* "But that's no reason for Parker to call you."

"You are a danger to society, Tobi. As the Chief of Police, I have a sworn duty to protect the citizens in my jurisdiction." Colbie recognized Parker Andrews, but she didn't know the man or woman standing to his side. Turning to her, Parker introduced Brinn Peters, a pretty brunette he said was also relatively new to the club. The man on Brinn's other side, stepped forward and held out his hand to her.

"It's nice to meet you, Colbie. I'm Dan Deal. I'm the club's resident psychologist. If you ever need someone to talk to, don't hesitate to give me a call." She wasn't sure why it surprised her that men who'd built such a successful kink club would keep a mental health professional on staff, but it did. When he laughed softly, Colbie realized the man was still holding her hand, and Bode was shooting daggers at the doctor with his eyes.

"Chill, Bode. The Wests pay me a substantial amount of money to make sure safe, sane, and consensual remain the guiding tenets of the Prairie Winds Club. I'm just doing my job." Tobi shifted from one foot to the other, and Dan shot her an indulgent smile.

"Tobi, I hear you had an exciting afternoon."

"Don't law enforcement and fire departments have some sort of confidentiality covenants or something?"

"You make them sound like monks or nuns, Tobi."

"That's convents, Gracie." Colbie looked at the other woman who'd stepped into their circle. Laughing when she realized Gracie also had two men standing directly behind her, Colbie felt at ease, despite the fact they were standing in a sex club.

"Well, we'd be better off with priests and nuns. They don't phone everyone they know every time you set off a little fire alarm." She shot a dark look at Parker which earned her a swat from Kyle, making her squeak.

Colbie watched the interplay between the club members gathered around them and before she could call the words back, she'd blurted out the question that kept dancing around in her mind.

"I notice a pattern here. Do all the women at this club have two Doms? Was there a buy one, get one free special or something?" When everyone around her froze, she silently prayed the floor would open up and swallow her whole. *I have got to get a damned filter installed between my brain and my mouth.*

Chapter Fifteen

LIAM THREW HIS HEAD back and laughed at Colbie's question. He'd been a member of the Prairie Winds Club for a year and had never questioned the number of polyamorous relationships. Hell, no wonder he loved this club so much. The members lived their lives unapologetically, and the local community didn't appear to care how many husbands a woman had as long as she was being treated well.

"No darlin'," Kent smiled at her and shook his head, "there are several traditional couples in the club, but my brother and I try to not make them feel like they're *different*."

"Oh yes, indeed," Micah Drake shook his head. "We all know Kyle is all about protecting everyone's feelings." Everyone laughed, and Liam watched as Colbie shook her head at the man's droll sarcasm.

"I think I'll pass on responding. It seems self-defeating to argue with the man who has information on everybody. The damn CIA calls him for information so often, I'm going to start billing them by the hour." Reaching in front of Tobi, he gave her nipple a quick pinch and grinned when she gasped. "Come on, Pet. I'm ready to play."

Watching his friends and their submissives drift in different directions, Liam looked down at Colbie and felt nothing but longing. He'd hoped she wouldn't be frightened or disgusted by what they wanted from her. Her easy acceptance of those involved in similar relationships had been a huge relief.

"Come on, Spitfire. Let's look around. We want to see what interests you." They'd already read her limit list, but it was obvious she hadn't planned to play at the club since she'd only filled in the bare minimum. He bet if they tried to negotiate some of the things she'd left on her list, she'd become much more interested in reviewing it.

Liam and Bode kept her between them as they moved to the side of the crowded room. They were standing in the shadows, but they weren't hidden from view. He and Bode positioned themselves between Colbie and the room, but she was still visible to anyone walking by closely. "I thought we were going to tour the club?"

"We are. But you aren't a complete newbie to the lifestyle, so we're going to up the stakes a bit."

This time it was Bode who pulled a black velvet bag from his pocket. Pulling open the drawstring top, he upended the contents into his palm and flashed a smile which made him look positively predatory. "Spread those lovely thighs, baby. These have been in my pocket so they're nice and warm. I'm going to make sure you're nice and wet before I slide them in. We'll tour the club until you're ready to go upstairs."

She spread her legs and her pupils dilated until there was nothing but a slim ring of blue circling them.

"What if I'm ready to go upstairs now?" The breathless quality of her voice went straight to his cock, and Liam had to fight the urge to shift himself away from the biting teeth of his zipper.

Liam couldn't see Bode's fingers, but he didn't need to—Colbie's body was telling him everything he needed to know. Her breathing quickened, and her barely audible mews were going to make him lose his mind. The glazed look moving over her face was the hottest thing he'd ever seen. When she began to sway on her feet, Liam moved behind her and wrapped an arm around her torso, lifting her breasts until they were practically spilling over the top of her dress.

"There's an incentive program, baby. Every ten minutes equal an orgasm you don't have to ask for. They'll be yours to take." Liam wanted to laugh at Bode's spur-of-the-moment *deal*. Colbie was competitive by nature; she would want to prove them wrong by winning, but she was already trembling in his arms. He could practically feel her resolve crumbling.

"As long as you don't try to indulge without one of us in the room." Liam wanted to make sure that was understood up front.

"Can't. Don't. My toys are gone." Liam wanted to laugh at her complaint about her pathetic sex toy collection. They'd tossed them all in the trash because there were so many better things available in the forum shops. "Oh. Oh, my heavenly stars and garters."

When her knees buckled, Liam had only let her fall a few inches, but feeling her small hands grasping his forearms—knowing she'd sought his support, was the best feeling in the world.

"I've got you, Spitfire. We'll always catch you."

"Let's go." Bode took her hand and tugged her along behind him like an errant child. Liam bit the inside of his cheek to keep from laughing out loud at his friend. The man whose reputation was heralded by Doms far and wide as a hard ass with submissives, was dangerously close to losing control, and Liam couldn't have been happier.

COLBIE TOOK SEVERAL quick steps before the vibrations from the balls Bode had slipped into her vagina registered in her brain. *Feathers!* The damned things were pressing against her G-spot. Her feet stopped so suddenly, you'd have thought they'd been bolted to the floor. Sucking in several deep breaths, she tried to focus on anything, but the sensation of heat igniting deep inside her core.

"Spitfire? Are you all right?" Liam's warm breath wafted over the shell of her ear, setting off another wave of heat which pushed her dangerously close to edge. *Don't come. Don't come. Don't come. You have to make it through at least one scene. Fucking hell, Colbie, get it together.*

"Yes. I'm okay. Mostly. It was just a surprise. Shock. Give me a second to…" She had to stop talking because her brain was rioting from the bombardment of sensations.

"Storeen, you haven't earned the right to come without permission, yet." Bode's words were enough to pull her back just enough for her temper to kick in. It didn't matter that it was probably exactly what he'd had in mind; she sucked in a couple of deep breaths, then nodded.

"I'm good. Let's go." The words had sounded much more convincing in her head, but it was too late for a do-over. His smug smile infused her with resolve. When she narrowed her eyes in defiance, he gave her ass a sharp swat that set the balls in motion again. *Blast him.*

"Glaring at your Dom is never a good idea, baby. Challenges will always be met." His tone was resolute, but she appreciated that he hadn't scolded her. Humiliation was never going to be an effective way to deal with her.

The first scene they watched was obviously meant to

be an introduction. Colbie struggled to hold back a yawn, it was so boring. The excitement building in her drained away before the Dom teasing his sub with an unimaginative assortment of toys managed to get the poor woman off. Colbie felt sorry for the young sub who looked disappointed, despite the smile she gave her Dom. Colbie noticed the frowns on Liam's and Bode's faces and looked at them in question.

"I hope the Dungeon Monitor standing over there takes that kid under his wing." Liam nodded to a guy whose black knit shirt was pulled so tight over his massive chest, she could see it rise and fall as he huffed out an exasperated breath.

"Somebody better or he's going to lose that sweet subbie who's trying so hard to smile, I'm afraid her teeth are going to crack." Colbie was grateful for the reprieve, but she felt sorry for the submissive. Bode turned to her and shook his head. "I'm sorry that scene was a bust. We knew the Dom was a new member, but he's not new to the lifestyle. I hope the little sub gives him another chance after the Dungeon Monitor coaches him a bit." She nodded, but was thinking the guy needed more than a little coaching.

Walking to the next scene wasn't nearly as torturous after their slow start. Colbie could feel the tension radiating from both men. She didn't want them to feel as if they'd let her down, but she also knew better than to pretend the incident hadn't happened. If they suspected she was faking arousal, there would likely be hell to pay. She'd seen that play out at Castle Masters and it hadn't been pretty.

"You're thinking too hard, Spitfire. What's going through that sharp mind of yours?" The opening Liam gave her was the perfect opportunity to turn the evening around… for herself and for them.

"I was just thinking how much I appreciated seeing how different it is here. Knowing the Dom will get some much-needed coaching, says a lot about the kind of club this is. And even though I know you think it was a bust, I still gained something from the experience." She took a deep breath to fortify her courage and then pulled them each down for a sweet kiss. "Thank you for not taking the easy way out and moving on right away. At least now, I might be able to get through at least one scene without melting into a puddle on the floor."

Liam and Bode both chuckled. "I do believe you missed your calling, Spitfire. You'd make one hell of a diplomat."

"Fucking hell. We're not letting those assholes in the Foreign and Commonwealth Office send her to the other side of nowhere. We're keeping her. Any woman who doesn't throw that disaster in our face is worth fighting for." Bode's vehemence surprised her, and the blistering kiss he gave her made her knees weak. *Big news, guys. You don't need hot scenes to wind me up.*

Chapter Sixteen

WALKING OFF THE ELEVATOR an hour later, Liam wondered how long he'd have the imprint of his zipper tattooed along the length of his cock. The last sixty minutes had been the longest of his life. Waiting for Colbie to tap out had turned out to be more of a test for him and Bode than it had been for her. He alternated between wanting to pin her against the wall and fuck her until she couldn't remember her own name and bending her over the nearest spanking bench to remind her she belonged to them. Even now, seeing the red imprint of his hand on her pretty ass appealed to him far more than it should.

Two steps into their living room, Bode turned and held up his hand to halt her progress.

"Where are the balls, Colbie?"

Liam leaned back against the wall as understanding dawned. She'd gone to the bathroom during the Wests' scene, and while he thought she acted odd when she returned, it hadn't occurred to him she would remove the balls.

Colbie's face turned crimson between one breath and the next, but to her credit she didn't look away. She looked Bode in the eye without blinking. "They're hidden in a vent in the locker room." For a split second, Liam was furious. Why would she be so underhanded? But something about the challenge in her eyes made him bite back the accusation.

"Explain." Liam knew that tone. Bode was angry, but he was keeping it carefully leashed—at least for now. When the flush on her face darkened, Liam realized it wasn't anger, but embarrassment coming off her in waves.

"They came out. I didn't take them out, I swear." She sucked in a deep breath as he and Bode stood silently waiting for her to continue. "For a couple of balls that wreaked so much havoc with my control, they were really small. And without being really graphic, I'll just say I lost them in the loo. Jen startled me when she pounded on the door in greeting... and well, never mind."

Liam glanced at Bode and saw the corners of his friend's mouth quiver as he tried valiantly to hold back his smile.

"It took the last bits of my self-control to fish them out. I was afraid they'd mess up the plumbing. I always forget American fixtures are more accommodating than those in Europe. Anyway, it turns out the sanitizer in the bathroom not only takes off germs. It eats plastic, too. Well, actually it doesn't actually eat it... more like chews it up and spits it back out. Jen tried to help me... after she stopped laughing. But we didn't have much time and for a locker room that puts most spas to shame, the place was totally lacking in useful tools."

Liam was a close as he'd ever been to losing control with a woman. The pictures flashing through his head reminded him of Lucy and Ethel in the old shows he'd seen on late night television. *This story had better end quickly, or I'm never going to be able to keep from laughing.*

SAM MCCALL HAD pulled Bode aside a few minutes ago and given him a heads up. The elder McCall had been laughing so hard, they'd had to step outside because they'd been drawing unwanted attention. Jen had confessed to Sam because she'd been worried Colbie would be in trouble. She'd begged her husband to intervene on her new friend's behalf, knowing there wasn't a chance in hell any Dom would fail to notice a couple of missing Ben Wa balls. Bode's temper had been close to boiling over when Sam had shaken his head.

"Listen, I understand why you're frustrated. She didn't tell you and probably should have, but take a minute and put yourself in her shoes. This is her first time at the club, and unless I'm misreading things, it's also the first time the three of you have played together in public. She's surrounded by people she only knows casually and obviously, wants to feel accepted. You haven't earned her trust as Doms, and we haven't earned her trust as friends."

As much as it galled him to admit it, Sam was right. When he finally blew out a breath, Sam smiled.

"It says a lot that she trusted Jen enough to enlist her help. If you go off half-cocked, you're going to throw Jen under the bus and that's not going to make anybody happy."

Bode wasn't a fool. He didn't want to piss off Sam or Sage, and he damned well didn't want to hurt Jen. She might look like a garden fairy, but it was a clever disguise. As near as he could tell, she was checking off all the boxes to become the first real-life, female superhero.

"Would you want to confess that fucking comedy in front of a bunch of near-strangers? Hell, even Jen pulled Sage and me aside to tell us. Think back... have you ever known her to be shy?"

Bode had finally laughed at the absurdity of the entire evening. The first scene they'd watched had been as bad as any he'd ever seen in a club. And now that he thought about it, Colbie had seemed skittish since returning from the locker room, but he'd assumed it was arousal. *Nothing arrogant about that, dumb ass.*

"Please tell Jen thanks. If we'd discovered the balls missing, we might not have been smart enough to listen to the explanation before saying a lot of shit we couldn't ever take back."

"I'll tell her," Sage nodded and slapped him on the back. "She's earned a reward, and I'm anxious to give it to her, so I'll leave you to sort this out with your woman. Remember, there's almost always more than one way to get where you want to be."

"I'm sorry." Colbie's whispered words brought him back to the moment, and he felt like an ass for becoming lost in the memory of his conversation with Sam. She'd obviously taken his silence as anger, and he couldn't blame her. Tears streamed down her face, and she looked close to imploding. Jesus, she'd had one hell of a night, and he was being a first-class ass. Liam was glaring at him. He had no defense.

"Come here." He didn't wait for her to take the steps to close the distance between them—pulling her into his arms and lifting her off her feet. "I wish you had told us, but I understand why you didn't. And I'm glad you enlisted Jen's help. She was worried about you, by the way. Liam and I will be sending her something special for her help." She sagged against him, and he finally chuckled. "Baby, you couldn't have picked a better partner in crime." *And this is a story that will probably become club lore by the end of the week.*

"Unless you'd partnered with Tobi. God knows this

sounds like the stories we've heard about her." Liam laughed and pulled her from Bode's arms into his own. "Did you ask to come up here because you were ready or because you were scared we were going to be angry?"

"I'd forgotten about it until we got on the elevator. The last scene pushed everything from my mind." Her admission sent a new surge of blood to his cock, and his waning erection was suddenly ready for action again. It must have had the same effect on Liam because he lifted Colbie into his arms and stalked down the hall, leaving Bode to follow him, chuckling at his friend's impatience.

COLBIE WASN'T SURE her legs were going to hold her up when Liam finally set her on her feet. She wobbled, but didn't collapse into a tangle of arms and legs on the floor, so she was calling it a win. The relief she felt when she realized they weren't angry with her had been staggering. She'd been fully prepared for them to lock her in the bedroom they'd given her and walk away.

Liam's green eyes watched her like a cat studying the mouse he'd finally cornered. "Whatever your thinking, push it out of your mind, right now. Nothing exists outside of this moment." His expression morphed into something slightly sinister, his smile reminding her of Snidely Whiplash. "And those freebie orgasms you earned downstairs? Gone. That's your punishment for not telling us what happened in the locker room."

She knew she should be grateful that was her only punishment, but she hadn't had an orgasm in so long which wasn't battery operated, she was worried she'd go off like a rocket the first time they touched her. Nodding her understanding earned her a scowl.

"Yes, Sir. I'm sorry I didn't tell you right away." Before she could add to her apology, Liam pressed his finger to her lips and shook his head.

"Let it go. Tonight is about pleasure—yours and ours, but that will change if you come without permission." This was the Dom side of Liam she'd only gotten glimpses of before. The charm was still there, but it's veneer was more transparent, giving her a closer look at the sexual dominant lurking just below the surface. "I see you drifting away, Spitfire. Let's see if I can't regain your undivided attention." The sound of rending fabric filled the room, and the dress they'd given her to wear slithered to the floor, pooling around her feet.

"Holy cat nip. I... well, I would have taken it off if you'd asked."

"YOU'RE GOING TO FIND we won't *ask* often, Storeen. In scenes, we'll command and you'll obey." Liam bit back his snort at Bode's declaration. They'd already told her they were bossy bastards, but they would limit it to sex unless it involved her safety—then all bets were off.

"Yes, Sir." *Smart girl.*

"Are you on birth control, Colbie?" They'd read her club file, and knew she'd taken birth control pills since her teens, but a lot could change in a year.

"Yes, Sir, and I'm clean. I haven't been with anyone in over... well, in a really long time." Liam saw Bode's brow raise in question.

"When was the last time you had sex, Colbie?" Liam kept his tone even despite his burning need to take apart any man who'd fucked her.

She didn't drop her gaze, but her cheeks flamed with embarrassment. Liam watched her take a steadying breath before answering.

"My junior year of college."

This time it was their turn to stare blankly at her. Liam was positively speechless. She'd started college two days after her fifteenth birthday. Which meant she hadn't had sex since she was seventeen. When neither of them responded, she blushed further.

"Actually, there wasn't much time between my first and last time. My body didn't like the latex condom and after the second try, I decided it wasn't worth it. I might have been gifted academically, but I didn't know you could get them without latex. Probably a good thing I didn't find that out until later."

Bode shook his head and gave her a wry grin. "We're both clean. We've got copies of the test results." Liam knew neither of them had fucked a woman without a condom since their early teens and just thinking about taking her bare made him desperate to shove himself so deep, he'd be able to feel her heart beating.

"I'd rather not use condoms. Thank you for offering to show me the test results, but I wouldn't be here if I didn't trust you."

"Up you go." Before she could say anymore, Bode lifted her onto the bed, directing her to scoot to the center and lay back against the pillows. Looking down on her, Liam wondered how they'd ever be able to go slow enough to make this a night she'd always remember.

Bode pulled his shirt over his head before moving to the head of the bed and sealing his lips over hers. Liam watched her body tense briefly before melting like butter under the heat of Bode's kiss. Stripping off his clothes before positioning himself between her legs, Liam inhaled the musky scent of her sex and twirled his fingers through the drenched folds.

"Your pussy is so wet, Spitfire. I'm going to coat my tongue with your sweet cream and then drive you right out of your mind before I push you over the edge." Her clit was already peeking out from under its hood, the pearly nub begging for his attention. Using his fingers to fully expose the sensitive bundle of nerves, Liam flicked his tongue over it and smiled at her keening cry. Using the pad of his middle finger, Liam pressed against her G-spot and groaned at the rush of cream coating his hand.

"You aren't going to believe how responsive she is. Every touch we give her makes the muscles lining her vagina clench so tight, I can barely move my finger."

"Oh, God. Please. I need more." The desperation in her voice was music to his ears, he was happy to step up his game. Pushing her thighs further apart with his shoulders, Liam told her to place her feet flat on the bed. This position lifted her ass enough he could slip a hand under her. It only took a few seconds for her natural lubrication to coat his finger enough he was able to begin massaging circles around the puckered muscle surrounding her rear hole.

"We'll fuck you here, Spitfire. One of us will be balls deep in your pussy while the other breaches your ass. You'll come so hard, you won't remember your own name."

Colbie's body shuddered, and he took advantage of her moment of distraction to breach her sphincter with the tip of his finger. She screamed, "Yes" at the same time Bode gave her permission to come. Liam fucked her with his curled tongue and nearly came himself when she shattered.

Her cries were muffled, telling him Bode had claimed her mouth in a kiss which sent a shudder through her entire body. Before she'd stopped writhing, he moved over her and pushed in to the hilt. He could feel the heat of her muscles stretching to accommodate him, and as much as he hated to admit it, he was as close to losing control of his own release as he'd been in decades.

"Now. Don't. Hold. Back." Colbie's staccato words were followed by a quick cant of her hips which pushed him almost all the way in.

"Hold still, Colbie. For fuck's sake I'm holding on by a thread. Your body isn't ready, I don't want to hurt you." It had been so long since Liam had been skin to skin during sex, his body was screaming to be let off the straining tether holding him back. His brain was drowning in desire; he didn't have a prayer of holding off for as long as he should.

"I can't. I need you to fuck me, or I'm going to die. Please, I'm begging you."

His control snapped like a brittle twig, and he set a quick pace that was never going to be mistaken for restraint.

"We'll do slow and easy next time. Maybe." Feeling the tip of his cock pushing against her heated cervix was taking him apart, one thrust at a time. In the distance, he heard Bode say something to her, but Liam couldn't make out the words over the sound of blood rushing in his ears. When the muscles lining her channel clamped down on him, fire shot up his spine as lightning flashed behind his eyelids, and the world exploded around him.

A few seconds later, Liam felt himself floating back to earth and realized his arms were trembling so violently, they were barely holding him up. Colbie's moan when he slipped from her as he rolled them to the side made his smile.

"Jesus, Joseph, and Mary, Spitfire, you melted my brain.

"I'll come up with something really clever and respond to that as soon as I find all the missing pieces of mine." Liam would have laughed at her response if he had the energy.

Chapter Seventeen

BODE HADN'T THOUGHT his dick could get any harder, but he'd been wrong. Watching Liam fuck Colbie had been the sweetest torture in the world. He'd peeled his pants off to keep from bursting out of them while she and Liam had been screaming out their releases. When his friend rolled her to the side, and she wiggled her perfect ass against his bare flesh, his cock zeroed in on the heat and before he knew what was happening, the tip was pressed against her opening. Gripping her waist to still her sexy little grinding movement, he groaned at the exquisite pleasure.

"Be still, baby. You're playing with fire, and my control is for shit after watching you two. Hell, I've seen some hot scenes, but damn. That's going to be burned in my memory until I take my last breath." The little imp arched her back pressing the tip of his cock into her heat.

"Yes. Bode. Sir. Please. I want you."

Bode felt his eyes roll back so far, he swore he could see the guy running his brain reach for the fire extinguisher. She was frying all his synapsis. Now he understood the stuck on stupid look on Liam's face.

"I'll go deeper at this angle, baby, are you sure you're ready?" He took his cock in his hand and moved it back and forth through her drenched folds, making sure he was well lubricated with her cream before pushing deep with one thrust of his hips. Liam lifted her leg, giving Bode better access and with the second thrust, he was balls deep with his tip nestled against her cervix. *Damn, she's so fucking tiny. I've got to be careful.*

"Yes. Ready. Go. Please. Now!" Colbie lost most of her leverage when Liam held her top leg and draped his own muscular calf over her bottom thigh. Just that small hint of bondage sent a shudder through her, and she went liquid around him.

"I think our woman is going to like being bound. We're going to have fun exploring that with her." The sound Colbie made was something between a whine and a moan, prompting Liam to give Bode a heated look. Oh yeah, he understood his unspoken words perfectly. Yes, Colbie was hot, and she thought she was ready for anything they could throw at her. But according to her file, she was an anal virgin. He was too far gone to give her the time she needed to prepare.

"It feels so good. So different. It's the position, isn't it?" He loved that she was able to differentiate between the ways her body responded, but she was thinking too damned much.

"You're right, little Spitfire, but Master Bode doesn't want you focused on *the why of things*. I assure you, he wants you to turn off that spectacularly brilliant mind and just feel."

"Let go, baby. Give yourself over to me. To us. The heart of submission is surrendering. Letting us take you where you need to be." She responded beautifully, softening in his arms, the rigidity of her muscles eased. "That's my girl. Take what I give you. If you'll open yourself to us, you'll discover we'll give you everything." With those words, he began a random pattern of thrusts. Some were pounding possession, others soft whispering slides filled with promise.

He loved hearing the mews and gasps when she'd anticipated a stroke and was surprised to receive one entirely different. Keeping her on edge long enough for her body to recover and ready itself for another earth-moving orgasm.

"Remember, submission can take many forms. The beauty of it is in the sincerity, not the severity. Seeing your eyes glaze over as your body releases its control into our hands is the most beautiful thing in the world, love. Watching you unravel for the first time with your other Master is a gift I'll always treasure. Come for him, Spitfire."

Colbie's vaginal walls tightened like a vice around Bode's cock, the rippling a prelude heralding her release. Bode hadn't been prepared for the intensity of the contractions; her orgasm triggered his. Christ in heaven, he couldn't even remember the last time he hadn't given a woman at least two orgasms before claiming his own. Grateful he was already laying down, Bode kissed the side of Colbie's neck where her pulse thundered just beneath the surface. It was good to know he wasn't the only one affected by the explosive sex they'd just shared.

"We're going to try that again in a few hours and see if we can't get it right. But first, I think we could all use some sleep."

"If it gets anymore *right*, I won't survive it." Her whispered words made Bode and Liam chuckle. Stumbling from the bed, Bode returned from the en suite with a warm washcloth. Gently washing the evidence of their joining from her made her grumble in her sleep. Patting the tender tissues dry, Bode looked at Liam and shook his head.

"Taking her bare completely blew my mind. I don't

think I'll ever be able to use a condom again." He hadn't fucked without protection since he too young to have been having sex and too naïve to understand the risks he was taking. Bode had always thanked God for protecting him when he'd been too dumb to protect himself.

"She's the one." Liam's eyes told him the point was no longer negotiable. Hell, Bode wasn't a fool, he knew there was no turning back now. The remnants of his good intentions and the tattered fragments of his arrogant plan to exercise caution had been blown to bits the minute she'd taken him into her exhausted body. She'd wanted him, but he knew she'd been exhausted. That hadn't stopped her from insisting, even though the most conceited bastard on the planet would have seen through her. Colbie hadn't wanted him to feel left out and pushed herself into a coma to see to it he'd gotten what he needed.

Flipping off the light and sliding beneath the covers, Bode moved to Colbie's side. A feeling of contentment he'd never experienced rolled over him when she turned to burrow closer. She hadn't been sleeping well; he was thrilled to know she was resting peacefully in his arms. Through the fog of sleep, Bode heard Liam's phone beep and then felt the bed shift. He wondered briefly where he'd left his own phone, but he wasn't going to disturb the sleeping angel in his arms, so the damned thing could stay wherever it was.

LIAM WAS TEMPTED to tuck his phone under the mattress or throw it out the nearest window. Would the damn thing ever stop vibrating on the bedside table? After a few seconds of blissful silence, the alarm beeped. There were only a handful of people who could activate the alarm and one of them was sleeping peacefully on the other side of the naked goddess beside him. Rolling gently away from Colbie's warmth, he tucked the blanket close to her, hoping she wouldn't notice he was gone. Grabbing his phone and a pair of pants, he stepped into the hall before answering.

"I'm sorry to disturb you, but you're going to want to hear this." Kyle West's voice was all business and Liam's FUBAR detector was pegging out. Something was fucked up beyond all recognition—the question was what? Walking in to the room where he'd slept for the past year, Liam smiled as he pulled clothes from the closet. He and Bode would be moving in to the master suite as soon as possible. No more lying alone in that damned bed, wondering what Colbie was doing and whether or not she was safe.

Walking into the club's conference room office ten minutes later, Liam was surprised to see several members of the team, steaming cups of coffee in hand, staring at a large wall monitor.

"Don't you people ever sleep? Vampires, the whole lot of you." Micah Drake was standing close enough to hear his muttering and snorted a laugh.

"I assure you I'm not a vampire. I need my beauty sleep, but the boss doesn't. We mortals suck down coffee by the gallon to keep up with him."

Kyle looked up and motioned him over. "A joint force unit raided a compound housing one of the world's biggest slave traders. The operation took place this morning, and they're just starting to go through the mountain of paper they found."

Micah walked up beside him and rolled his eyes. "This

guy was either a technophobe or the world's biggest idiot. From the chatter I'm hearing, there are details on every kid they've ever taken off the street, including buyers and prices."

Kyle nodded. "The good thing is, they know where to start looking for these kids. But when word leaks out about this, every one of their lives will be in danger. The clock is ticking, which means numerous intelligence organizations are scrambling to get teams dispatched to rescue as many of the victims as they can."

Liam understood what Kyle was trying to avoid saying aloud. There was just too much money to be made selling the intel. And even the most prestigious groups had members who could be compromised if the price was right. No one liked to acknowledge it, but that didn't change the reality.

"This is good news for Colbie, but I have a feeling there's something I haven't heard yet." This wasn't anything they couldn't have told him in the morning, so Liam felt like he was waiting for the other shoe to drop.

"You're right, there's more." Kyle sighed and ran his hand through his hair—a move Liam had come to know meant the former Navy SEAL was frustrated and nearing the end of his patience. "One of the first reports to come out on the paperwork involves a planned hit—on Colbie. Once they tracked her down, the man in charge planned to make good on his vow to make an example of her. You remember what he did to the two guys she overheard— hell, I don't think I'll ever get those pictures out of my head."

Liam still saw their charred bodies hanging in a tree, mouths open in silent screams. Thinking about those barbarians getting their hands on Colbie made Liam see red. This is why the sniper hadn't taken a kill shot, he'd wanted to bring her in for the boss to... Shit, Liam didn't even want to think about what they had planned for her.

"Fuck. What a mess. It's a Catch-22 from hell." It was still a hit, even if it was a kidnapping. The only way to dissuade the pricks trying to take her was to let them know they weren't going to be paid, but putting the word on the street endangered countless other people who were being held as sex slaves and subjected to unspeakable horrors.

"Exactly. We've got to double down on her protection." Kyle paused and Liam watched as he appeared to wage some sort of internal struggle. "Listen, I don't want to sound like an ass." Howling laughter from the door had everyone in the room turning to see Kent West moving to his brother's side.

"Don't give up something you're good at, brother. Just tell him straight up. If we lock Colbie down, she'll pull a Tobi, and that'll make her twice as hard to protect. Go ahead, tell him, I wouldn't want to steal your thunder." Everybody thought Kent was the more affable of the two men, but Liam had seen them trade that title back and forth so often, he wasn't convinced it belonged to either of them.

"Somebody's going to shoot your mouthy ass someday, just on principle." Kyle's words lacked any real conviction, and Kent's unrepentant grin had most of the team members chuckling as they returned to their own conversations. "As my brother already so ineloquently said, I'm worried we've already restricted her as much as we dare. She's already been injured while staying on-site. If we try to keep her inside, she's apt to say *screw it* and take off."

She had the financial resources to run. Liam knew she'd been living hand-to-mouth because she hadn't wanted to touch the money from her trust fund, but that didn't mean she couldn't have a couple hundred thousand in her pocket by tomorrow night. The last time he'd checked, the account had mushroomed to the point a half-mil gone would barely be noticed.

"The good news is one of the two men who were asking about Colbie that day at Gus' was picked up last night at LaGuardia before he could board a red-eye flight to London." Kyle didn't seem convinced that was going to help much, and Liam agreed.

He agreed to discuss it with Bode while the ladies were busy at the spa. Rubbing his forehead, he couldn't believe he had to be out of bed for an early morning training session in a couple of hours. *I'm getting too old for this shit.*

Chapter Eighteen

COLBIE STARED AT her reflection in the mirror before looking up at the woman who'd spent hours adding extensions to her hair. When tears filled her eyes, the young hairdresser's eyes went glassy, as well, as she bit her lip.

"You don't like it? I'm sorry, we can cut it again." *Good job, Colbie. Hurt the poor girl's feelings with your stuck on stupid response.*

"No. I love it. It's just... well, I haven't seen that woman in a long time. I was surprised and relieved. To be honest, I was terrified I'd lost her forever." Colbie saw the girl sag with relief as Tobi and Gracie burst into the room.

"Holy shit, TJ." The little miracle worker went rigid again, and Colbie laughed.

"Tobi, I scared her by not saying anything and now you're doing the same by not elaborating."

"Oh, damn. Sorry. You are one amazing hairdresser. We're keeping you." Turning to the hallway, she shouted to no one in particular, "Don't anybody let my husbands scare TJ off. She's a Mensa level hair whisperer, and we're keeping her." TJ's face turned crimson, but her ear to ear smile was filled with pride.

"This calls for a celebration. Margaritas and snacks by the pool ladies, let's go. I'm starving. Having the hair on my pink bits yanked out by its roots is exhausting." Gracie shuddered as they headed for the door.

Colbie turned around and gave TJ a hug of thanks before running to catch up with her friends. The blonde extensions were straighter than her natural hair, but it didn't matter. For the first time in a year she felt like herself. Gracie was right. It was time for a little liquid celebration, and she loved margaritas.

Twenty minutes later, they sat by the sparkling pool enjoying the way the late afternoon sunshine made the water look like it was decorated with floating diamonds. It seemed odd for it to be so warm this late in the year, but Colbie wasn't complaining, she loved being outside breathing the fresh air. Colbie had already downed her first margarita and was halfway through her second when the conversation turned to Colbie's plan to work in the Prairie Winds garage. Tobi explained their hope to expand their business, but the two women confessed they hadn't hit on an idea they liked yet.

"Maybe you should add garage service for the submissives at the club? The Doms would know their subs weren't being taken advantage of, and they could spend time shopping at the forum shops or at the spa while they waited."

Tobi dropped the chip she was holding, and Gracie pushed her gargantuan sunglasses up on top of her head. Both women stared at her, jaws dropped almost to their chests; Colbie started to fidget under their scrutiny.

"What? It's not *that bad* of an idea."

"No, it's not bad at all, Colbie. It's fucking brilliant." Gracie winced at Tobi's curse, but nodded in agreement at the same time.

"It really is an amazing idea. I keep running it through my head and can't find any negatives. Having a female mechanic would be a huge draw; most women hate taking their car in because male mechanics don't take us seriously."

"No kidding. I haven't found one yet who knows what a whatchamacallit is. How is that even possible? How has any man gotten to be an adult without hearing his mother, grandmother, sister, girlfriend, or the even the neighbor lady use that term? Baffling." Tobi's observation was amusing, but it was also dead on. Colbie had seen the way some of the mechanics at Gus' rolled their eyes about the ladies' descriptions of their car problems. Their condescending attitudes were never appreciated by their female patrons.

"Colbie, would you be interested in this... as a partner, if we can work out the details?" Gracie's question surprised her, but she was suddenly thrilled with the idea. As the two women chattered a mile a minute about business plans and marketing strategies, Colbie stared into the distance, lost in thought. Movement on top of what the men had referred to as "the tower" caught her eye.

Tobi must have followed her line of sight, because she laughed. "Oh, holy hotcakes, Jen's practicing her ninja sniper skills. Kyle said Kip Morgan's wife, Caila, was flying in today to coach her. You really have to see the irony in that. Caila's a vet and an avid hunter." When Colbie and Gracie stared at her in confusion, Tobi shook her head. "I got those same dumbfounded looks from my husbands. I swear, Lilly is the only one who gets my humor anymore."

"And that scares the rest of us to death." Gracie's droll tone made Colbie snicker. "Speaking of Lilly, where is she? I thought she was joining us today?"

"Dean and Del were going across the river to work on the corner posts for the security fence, and she wanted to go along. She's got a new shotgun and is convinced there will be rattlesnakes to use for target practice." Tobi had barely finished speaking when two thunderous booms filled the air.

For a few seconds, Colbie wasn't sure where the sound had come from because it seemed to echo all around them. Tobi screamed and dove under the glass table pulling Gracie and Colbie with her. The reverberations from what sounded like a canon had barely subsided when they heard two cracks that sounded like firecrackers. Looking to the river, Colbie saw rock fragments from the cliff on the other side of the river flying through the air before falling toward the river. They were too far to hear the rocks splashing into the water, but a dull thud coming from that direction made Colbie shiver.

Suddenly, the irony of hiding under a glass table seemed like the funniest thing in the world. Colbie had enough to drink she couldn't hold back her hysterical laughter. Reaching up over the edge of the table and grabbing her drink, Colbie lifted the soon to be empty glass to her friends. "Here's to finishing this before the Queen's Regiment gets here. No way in Hampton they'll let me step to bick ub my brink."

"Oh dear. Tobi, did you mix the drinks?" Gracie's concern would have seemed a lot more legitimate without the cheesy grin, but then who was Tobi to complain when she was laughing like a loon, too?

"Yes, indeed. And they're mighty tasty, too, if I do say so myself. She's right, it would be a shame to see them go to waste." She'd grabbed the two glasses above her head. Both women drained their glasses as shouts came from the other side of the fence.

"We're gonna catch hell about hiding under a glass table. See through. Shattering glass. Cutting hazard. And probably a dozen other things I haven't thought about." Tobi slid her glass over by Colbie, but it was too late.

Kyle pulled Tobi from under the table at the same time Micah lifted Gracie to her feet. Bode and Liam both helped Colbie up.

"Pet, I saw that. And what the fuck are you doing hiding under a glass table. You're completely visible and have you considered how badly you could be hurt by glass raining down on you?"

All three women exchanged knowing looks and burst into laughter.

PARKER HAD IMMEDIATELY responded to Kyle's request for back up. When he'd heard the danger Colbie was in, he'd sent officers to watch the front of the Prairie Winds compound and called the local Parks and Wildlife office to ask for their help patrolling the river running the length of the back of the property.

Lead officer Bud Cartwright was also a member of the club, so he'd been the obvious choice to patrol the waterfront. The second officer looked so young, Parker wondered how he'd ever passed the background check. After briefing both men, they made their way down river, and the younger man surprised him when he said he'd met Colbie.

"Damn, that gal is one hell of a mechanic. You need your hunting rifle fixed or fine-tuned? I'm your guy. But figure out what's clicking in the motor of my truck? I'm lost. The guys at Gus' always give me shit about not knowing anything about motors, but not Colbie. She was so polite and solved the problem in less than a day. Now, my girlfriend takes her car to Gus', too. Of course, she calls in advance to make sure Colbie has an opening, and the word's spreading through Darla's friends, too."

Parker smiled at Officer Tad Wesley's enthusiasm and watched as the other man moved to the forward deck of the boat, pole in hand to watch for shallow rocks. Large boulders sometimes fell from the rock cliff bordering the opposite side of the river from the Wests' property, causing a hazard to boats if their drivers didn't stay alert. Parker stepped forward from the aft deck to the pilot house to talk to Gus when all hell broke loose.

Kyle had warned him that his mom had a new shotgun and was helping her husbands high above the river, so the two booming shotgun blasts weren't a complete surprise. But the screaming man who launched himself over the top of the cliff would have been almost comedic if he hadn't landed on the deck with a sickening thud.

Tad jumped under the boat's canopy, his eyes so wide they looked like dark frisbees. He looked at Bud who's half-grin was typical of his laid-back nature. Bud nodded in the direction of the fallen man as he deadpanned.

"I heard Miss Lilly got a new shotgun." His chuckle was contagious, and Parker found himself shaking his head.

"Holy crap, Lilly West? I've heard about her. Damn, this is gonna be a tale and a half. But who was shooting the high-power from that tower?" *High-power? Tower?* From the forward deck, Tad would have had a clearer view, and he'd obviously heard something Parker hadn't. *Christ, I'll never get finished with the mountain of paperwork headed my way.*

An hour later, Parker rubbed his forehead in frustration. Kyle had convinced him to move the investigation to the conference room at the club, so they could better protect Colbie—the fewer people who connected her to the day's events, the better.

Lilly West sat regally across from him, every inch the poised beauty queen she'd once been. She looked between her husbands and shrugged.

"I don't know what all the fuss is about. Everybody gets in a snit when I shoot people, but I didn't shoot that man... he jumped. I didn't even see his gun until he pointed it at me. I really should have let the snake bite him, it would have served him right."

"That snake is now in ten million pieces, love. He won't be biting anyone. And the next time some fucker points a gun at you, don't you be hesitating to shoot him. My brother and I will take care of anybody bitching about it." Del West gave his wife a quick kiss before turning his attention to Parker. "You about finished up with us, Parker? Your deputies retrieved the guns that fellow had, but they didn't seem interested in collecting any of the snake bits."

"I tried to tell them it was evidence, but they didn't listen to me." Dean West's grin was pure orneriness. Parker suddenly had a vision of Kyle in a few years. Parker was probably going to have to beg his deputies to not quit after they'd spent time with the Wests up on top the cliff. Their blasé attitude about a hired hitman jumping off a cliff to his death would most likely shock those who didn't know them.

Fighting back his own amusement at the mental picture he'd drawn of the last moments of the jumper's life, Parker shook his head. The poor bastard must have thought Lilly was going to shoot him when she'd walked up on where he lay, taking aim at Colbie. The damned guns they'd found in the grass were long-range; from

Parker's viewpoint, the guy meant business, this time. It would have been damned entertaining to have seen the look on his face when the shooter noticed the rattler inches from his crotch. According to Lilly, he'd scrambled over the edge just as she'd blown the snake to hell.

"When am I going to get my new gun back? Parker, don't you dare tell me it's being held as evidence when shooting rattlesnakes isn't against the law."

Parker sighed. "Kyle locked it in the safe and..."

"That was just mean, Parker. I really would have expected better of you." The glare she'd given him would melt steel. He barely held back his cringe at the reprimand. Turning to Del, she smiled sweetly as she patted his cheek, "Darling, you'll make Kyle give me my gun back, won't you? You know how he gets. I just don't understand why those boys think they can boss around their mama." *Jesus, I'm going to get a cavity if I don't get her out of here.*

Chapter Nineteen

JEN PROPPED HER booted feet up on the chair next to her and looked at Caila Morgan. "I can't believe I missed him." Her shot had only been a fraction of a second late, but she might as well have not taken it at all because she'd missed her target by a couple of feet thanks to his backwards swan dive off the cliff. She'd heard the booming shots from Lilly's gun just before the man they'd been watching sailed backward into the air. They hadn't been able to see Lilly walking up on the sniper nestled in the grass until it was too late. Hell, they'd only sighted him a few seconds before Lilly's first shot.

"Well, it's not like we were expecting him to jump off the damned cliff. Cut yourself some slack. It takes practice to hit a moving target." Caila was slumped down on the sofa, downing her third ginger ale.

"You winged him."

"Yeah, but I've been hunting since I was old enough to carry my own gun. Besides, in the end it didn't matter. Dumb bastard killed himself when he landed face down on that boat." Jen shuddered at Caila's matter-of-fact description. She'd only seen the damage through the scope on her rifle, but that had been enough.

"Cripes, don't remind me. That was gruesome." The truth was, Jen was rethinking the sniper section of her resume. She wasn't cut out for the knowledge she'd ended someone's life when they hadn't been a direct threat to her. Shooting targets was one thing, shooting another person was an entirely different matter.

"Taking bets on how long it takes Kip to get here?" Caila grinned. "The Morgan brothers were finally starting to call me Caila again. Now I'm going to be right back to Calamity, you just watch and see. And this one wasn't my fault… not even a little."

"But you're a magnet for calamities, my little Mistress of Mayhem." Jen grinned at Kip Morgan who'd been standing behind his wife for several minutes. Caila squealed and turned to launch herself into his arms. "They did call me, but I was already on my way. As soon as we heard you and Jen were teaming up, and there were weapons involved, Sage had me on the first plane they could get ready for takeoff."

Caila was smothering Kip with kisses. Jen giggled when she saw his gaze land on the cans of ginger ale on the table beside his petite bundle of mischief. Damn, she liked Caila and had hoped to spend some more time with her, but she knew as soon as the Morgan men figured out what Jen already suspected, they were going to drop a net over her.

Kip leveled a look at Jen, raising a brow in question. She simply grinned and shrugged. *Not ratting out a sister. Sorry buddy, that big bad Dom look doesn't scare me, I've got two at home.*

"Jen, you're free to go. Preliminary ballistics indicate the bullet in the victim's shoulder didn't come from your gun." Parker stood with his arms crossed over his massive chest, glaring at her from across the room.

"I could have saved you the trouble of the test. I knew I missed, but thanks for announcing it to the masses, Parker." They might be in the club, but only because his damned office wasn't secure enough for any investigation related to Colbie, so she didn't give two shits about protocol. He might be a Dom, but he'd been an ass since she and Caila had been unceremoniously dumped in Kyle's office hours ago. Hell, one of his deputies had even escorted Caila on each of her two dozen trips to the bathroom.

"Be careful, kitten. All that hissing will be seen as a challenge." Sage's voice started her, but she should have known he wouldn't be far away. When she looked up at him, his grin made her heart melt. God, she loved her men so much, it sometimes scared her. He winked and then leaned down close enough to whisper against her ear. "And you know how much it turns me on when you *push*."

"Come on. Let's go. Where's Sage?" Jen was on her feet and tugging him to the door before her brain noticed her feet were moving. The room erupted in laughter as they walked out, but she didn't care. Sage wasn't the only one who could meet a challenge.

TOBI SNICKERED AT COLBIE'S futile effort to get Bode to retrieve their unfinished pitcher of margaritas from the outside table. Colbie turned to her and glared.

"See? I told you. I think it's in the Queen's Code of Conduct... don't let potential murder victims finish any drink that has a little paper umbrella in it. That might include fruit on sticks, too. I'm not sure. I'll have to get back to you on that part."

"Holy hell, sister, you're a hoot. We really do have to finish our conversation about the garage." Tobi saw Bode's puzzled look, but waved him off. "It's business. Nothing to worry your pretty little head about, sweetie." Gracie's howling laughter from beside her sent Tobi into a fit of giggles. "God, it did my heart good to say that to someone else. If I had a dollar for every time I've heard that, I'd thumb my nose at those mega-million lottery commercials."

"Kitten, you are skating on thin ice." The amusement in Kent's voice wasn't a deterrent, but she tried to act repentant. From the laughter surrounding her, Tobi assumed she should probably scrap her plan to take up acting.

"It's the tequila. Gracie's a terrible influence." Gracie's horrified gasp next to her sent Tobi into another fit of laughter. Colbie was wiping her eyes as the men stared at the three of them with barely restrained frustration.

"A bad influence? Girl, you're one to talk. Who made those tequila grenades, anyway? Wasn't me!" Gracie gave Tobi a shove with her shoulder and laughed. "Holy hell, who gave Lilly a cannon? Damn, that was loud. And that guy screaming all the way down like a fourteen-year-old girl. Kind of a fitting end to his pansy-ass if you ask me."

Colbie's snort of laughter was the only sound in the room for several seconds before Tobi joined in.

"I've been telling everyone you had a ruthless streak, but no one believed me. Damn, I hope one of Micah's ten zillion cameras caught that. I'm saving it forever!"

"I'm not ruthless, I just believe in karma." Gracie's faux indignation made Colbie smile.

Tobi yawned and stretched her legs. "I'm tired. I'm going"

"Nowhere." Kent's hand on her shoulder pressed her gently back down. "You're not going anywhere alone until they finish interrogating the pickup guy. He's a local kid and doesn't appear to be involved, but we aren't taking any chances."

"So, the bad guy hires some trusting kid to give him a ride to the airport and doesn't bother to mention he's planning to shoot Colbie on the way. Nice."

"I think I should be insulted at the casual way you put that out there, but I'm having trouble getting there. Probably because the tequila is wearing off, and that's a pity." Looking up at Bode, Colbie batted her eyes so dramatically, Tobi had to slap her hand over her mouth to keep from laughing. "Seems a pity to waste a half pitcher of margaritas. I mean... there are starving children in... oh, wait, that's not quite right."

LIAM MOVED IN front of Colbie and shook his head at her adorable confusion. "You look lovely, Spitfire. I'm looking forward to finding out what other services you enjoyed at the spa." His little head was already imagining how her silky-smooth pussy was going to feel against his tongue. "Since we don't have to leave the building, we're free to go." She surprised him by jumping to her feet and nodding.

"Yes, let's go. It's been an interesting day. Strangers smearing wax on my pink bits and then yanking out hair by the roots. Hours in a chair getting my long hair back though, that was totally worth it. A half-wasted pitcher of margaritas Bode won't let me go get, and some ass-hat who wanted to shoot me doing a swan dive off a cliff."

"Spitfire, I promise we'll make sure the end of your day is memorable enough to make everything else fade to a distant memory."

Epilogue

Six months later

COLBIE LEANED HER HIP against the desk she rarely used and looked out from the glass-enclosed crow's nest of the newly expanded Prairie Winds garage. All the bays were filled and the mechanics busy with a variety of cars as they worked to get things wrapped up before the end of the day. It was mid-afternoon on Friday, and she'd encouraged them to have everything out the door before they closed for the weekend.

The past six months had been hectic to say the least, and Colbie was grateful things finally appeared to be leveling out. She'd been involved in every aspect of the building's renovation and was continually amazed by how quickly the Wests could get things done. Working with Tobi and Gracie was fun and challenging, both women processed information at the speed of light and could be difficult to keep up with. Their longtime friendship enabled them to communicate in a form of verbal shorthand that often bewildered those around them. But the two entrepreneurs had taken Colbie's idea and run full-steam ahead with it.

Colbie had finally tapped into her untouched trust fund when she became a partner in Tobi's and Gracie's consulting business. It made her smile to think about her parents' money being used to set up a garage. In the end, they'd funded the very thing they'd wanted to keep her away from the most. The irony of that had been the topic of a recent poolside discussion between Colbie and the men who now owned her heart.

Strong arms encircled her, and Colbie didn't have to look to recognize Liam's touch. "What had you so lost in thought you didn't hear me come up behind you, Spitfire?"

"I'm getting married tomorrow. Joining my life with the two most amazing men in the world. I think that gives me reason enough to be distracted." Actually, she'd done very little of the wedding planning. Lilly West had been thrilled when Colbie asked for her help. She'd taken on the project with an enthusiasm that humbled Colbie and taken the sting out of not having her own mother nearby during what should have been a joyous occasion they could share.

The death of the man who'd vowed to make an example of her had given Guinevere Colbert-Lister the opportunity to return to her previous life. But Colbie Clark had decided what she had now was so much *more*, and she'd been unwilling to give it up. MI6 agents had gone to her parents and explained the situation, but they'd expressed little interest in reconnecting with her. She'd be lying if she said it hadn't hurt, but she had too much to be thankful for to focus on what she'd lost.

As if he'd read her thoughts, Liam leaned down and gently bit down on her ear. "My parents are thrilled to be getting a daughter, Spitfire." His fingers traced over the diamond and platinum collar she wore, bringing a flood of memories about the night she'd stood naked in front of their friends and pledged her heart to Liam and Bode. In her mind, her vow to belong to them, to trust them with her body and soul, was every bit as important as those she would make tomorrow. Each ceremony would hold an important place in her heart.

"Did you get them settled into their hotel?" Lilly had offered to host both families, but Liam's and Bode's families insisted on staying at a nearby hotel. The last Colbie had heard, they'd reserved every room in the entire facility.

Liam chuckled, the rumbling against her back making her wish they didn't have to leave in the next few minutes for the rehearsal.

"Don't even think about skipping rehearsal." Tobi's voice came from behind them, and Colbie suddenly wondered if there wasn't a serious design flaw in the room she called her office. "Lilly will go bananas."

"And no one wants that. People get blown up and jump off cliffs," Gracie giggled from behind Tobi. Colbie couldn't hold back her own laughter any longer.

"Parker made us promise to keep her away from anything with a firing pin this weekend, but I think that's an unreasonable request." Kent walked in, and suddenly Colbie was wondering how many others were going to file into the rapidly shrinking space.

"I got her a white satin fanny pack and decorated it with lace and pearls. I'm telling you... that thing must weigh ten pounds. She's filled it with everything you'd need to survive a nuclear holocaust. J-Lo in *The Wedding Planner* has nothing on her." Tobi's laughter was contagious, and Colbie felt some of the tension drain from her shoulders as the banter continued. She just needed to make it through the next thirty-six hours, then the three of them would have two full weeks to themselves.

COLBIE CURTSIED AT the end of the waltz she'd shared with Liam and laughed when he turned her into Bode's waiting arms. The traditional service had been for the public and Liam's parents, who didn't know about their son's polyamorous relationship. Bode's parents had attended both the church ceremony and the joining. Colbie found it amusing that the two couples had been longtime friends, but Benjamin and Carolyn James seemed blissfully unaware of Oliver and Elizabeth Ford's D/s relationship.

The late afternoon church service had been elegant and a dream come true for Colbie. Beautiful white flowers were almost luminescent in the flickering candlelight. She'd cried when Bode sang Elvis Presley's, *I Can't Help Falling in Love*. His deep voice filled her heart with joy as the underlying message settled around her. It was perfect, but the private ceremony in the Wests' office held the most meaning for her. The joining ceremony had been performed by a member of the club, and his words had woven a magical spell, linking their hearts for eternity.

"What are you thinking about that's put that smile on your face, wife?" Bode might have smiled as he asked, but Colbie wasn't naïve enough to believe it was really a question.

"Well, handsome husband, I was thinking about what an amazing day we've had, and how much I'm looking forward to our honeymoon." Colbie felt Bode stiffen against her and pulled back to look at him just as he spoke.

"What the hell?" Colbie followed his line of sight to the door. She recognized the petite blonde as Dr. Tally Tyson, Senator Karl Tyson's widow; she'd seen the woman on television several times since her husband's plane had crashed, almost a year ago, in South America. Colbie didn't know the man talking animatedly to Kyle West, but his possessive hold on the trembling woman left little doubt about their intimate relationship. "Come on, let's see what this is about."

As they approached the rapidly growing group surrounding the table where the Senator's pale and clearly shaken wife was now seated, Colbie noticed the surface was covered with photographs.

"Koi, have you contacted any of your former contacts in the Agency?" Kyle West asked.

When Colbie finally managed to push her way closer, her mind tried to make sense of what she was seeing. A man, barefoot and wearing what appeared to be the tattered remnants of clothing, stared blankly into space. He was chained to a large post in the middle of what looked like a grass hut with a dirt floor. She'd been so riveted to the man's lost expression, the words written along the bottom of the photograph hadn't registered until the doctor's trembling fingers traced a line beneath the two words Colbie knew had rocked the other woman's world.

He's alive.

The End

Books by Avery Gale

The Wolf Pack Series
Mated – Book One
Fated Magic – Book Two
Tempted by Darkness – Book Three

Masters of the Prairie Winds Club
Out of the Storm
Saving Grace
Jen's Journey
Bound Treasure
Punishing for Pleasure
Accidental Trifecta
Missionary Position
Another Second Chance

The ShadowDance Club
Katarina's Return – Book One
Jenna's Submission – Book Two
Rissa's Recovery – Book Three
Trace & Tori – Book Four
Reborn as Bree – Book Five
Red Clouds Dancing – Book Six
Perfect Picture – Book Seven

Club Isola
Capturing Callie – Book One
Healing Holly – Book Two
Claiming Abby – Book Three

The Knights of the Boardroom
Book One
Book Two
Book Three

The Morgan Brothers of Montana
Coral Hearts – Book One
Dancing with Deception – Book Two
Caged Songbird – Book Three
Game On – Book Four
Well Bred – Book Five

Mountain Mastery
Well Written
Savannah's Sentinel
Sheltering Reagan

I would love to hear from you!

Website:
www.averygalebooks.com/index.html

Facebook:
facebook.com/avery.gale.3

Twitter:
@avery_gale

Made in the USA
San Bernardino, CA
30 April 2018